Women's Minyan

Also by Naomi Ragen

Naomi Ragen

WOMEN'S MINYAN

The Toby Press

The Toby Press LLC, 2006

POB 8531, New Milford, CT 06776-8531, USA
& POB 2455, London W1A 5WY, England
www.tobypress.com

First Edition

All professional inquiries in regard to this play should
be addressed to the author, naomi@naomiragen.com,
POB 23004, Jerusalem, 91230, Israel

ISBN 1 59264 156 3, *paperback*

A CIP catalogue record for this title is
available from the British Library

Photographs by Gérard Allon

Typeset in Garamond by Jerusalem Typesetting

Printed and bound in the United States
by Thomson-Shore Inc., Michigan

for Rachel Schapira

Foreword

Women's Minyan was inspired by the true life story of an ultra-Orthodox Jewish woman in Jerusalem who was forcibly separated from her twelve children by a vengeful ex-husband and a complacent and corrupt social and judicial system. When Women's Minyan premiered, this woman hadn't seen her children for five years. It has now been ten years. While her case has been taken to Israel's Supreme Court, it is doubtful she will ever see them again in her lifetime.

Her story is not unique to her, nor to ultra-Orthodox Judaism. The pattern of abuse towards women emanating from the fundamentalist religious sects of all religions—all of whom profess to serve a just and compassionate God—is frighteningly similar all over the world. The solution will come when women, particularly religious women, refuse to accept these abuses against their sisters, standing together to change the world, looking to the true God for their inspiration and their courage.—NR

Author's Preface

The play *Women's Minyan* takes place in the contemporary world of *haredim* or ultra-Orthodox Jews, who are themselves subdivided into many warring groups and sects. The literal meaning of *haredi* is: "One who quakes with fear of God." Dress and behavior in the *haredi* world are severely circumscribed by stringent laws and customs for both men and women, whose lives are centered around prayer, and the study of Talmud in yeshiva. It is a patriarchal society in which women's place is clearly delineated. Women marry in their late teens in arranged marriages. Birth control is frowned upon and large families the norm. Twelve children are not unusual. Women work outside the home to support the family so as to allow their husbands to continue as full-time Talmud students. This is considered a woman's achievement and her honor. The dress code for women is unbending in its adherence to modesty. All the characters are dressed in high-necked, long sleeved, mid-calf clothing, with slight variations that reveal status and character. All married women hide their hair under headcoverings that range from a simple scarf, to an elaborate pointed turban, or wig. The type and quality of headcovering reveals their status.

Except for Zehava who is Sephardi, i.e. a Jew of North African or Middle Eastern origin, all the women are Ashkenazim—Jews of Eastern European ancestry. In the *haredi* world, Sephardim are considered to be of inferior social status.

Fruma Kashman is both an enforcer and a victim of a social system in which religion is used to grind down a person's sense of self-worth, leaving them open to manipulation and recruitment into the faceless ranks of unquestioning followers, who don't dare question their charismatic leaders. She is a person who has abdicated her moral responsibility to judge right from wrong. At times, this leads her to truly evil deeds.

Tovah Klein works at the ritual baths, *mikvah,* a place where women are required to perform a monthly ablution seven days after the completion of their menstrual period, and before being allowed to resume relations with their husband. The taboo against sexual relations during this time period is severe, the punishment for trangression amounting to one's being cut off from God and the Jewish people. She is a sternly pious woman whose job it is to check over women's bodies—to see if they've cut their nails short enough, scrubbed their skin hard enough, taken off all make-up and jewelry—before allowing them to immerse in the waters. Most of her time is spent determining if everyone conforms to the written and unwritten rules of the ultra-Orthodox world, which will allow them to remain members in good standing of the community. Women like her rule with an iron hand, and a wagging tongue.

The opening lines spoken by MALE VOICE are a verbatim quotation from a contemporary book of Jewish law. The term *minyan* literally means a quorum of ten men, which is considered the smallest number comprising a congregation which has the authority to hold public prayer services, and decide other communal acts. The title, *Women's Minyan*, is meant to be ironic and defiant, because women have no status or authority in the public sphere in the ultra-Orthodox, *haredi,* world. Women cannot constitute a *minyan*.

DIRECTORS PLEASE NOTE: The men in this play must never, under any circumstances, be visible to the audience in any way. Their invisibility is extremely important both symbolically and dramatically. They permeate a *haredi* woman's life even when they are not physically present, and the hurtful epitaphs they sling lead to emotional overload and a fatal refocusing of the play when they appear on stage in any way.

Further note: the male voice of authority at the beginning must never be confused with the subsequent male voices who hurl insults at Chana. The former is the voice of the Rabbi, the latter the voice of the street hoodlums.

Yiddish terms are followed in brackets by their English translations. Some Yiddish terms will be familiar to English-speaking audiences, as such terms as *meshugah* and *chutzpah*, which have become part of American speech. Others may be less familiar. The director is free to choose among them, or use the English translation. It is suggested that the term *Ima,* meaning mother, be used throughout by Bluma and Shaine Ruth when they address or refer to their mother.

—NR

CHANA SHEINHOFF
SHAINE RUTH
BLUMA
GOLDIE SHEINHOFF
ADINA SHEINHOFF
FRUME KASHMAN
GITTE LEAH KASHMAN
ETA LEIBOWITZ
TOVAH KLEIN
ZEHAVA TOLEDANO
TWO YOUNG GIRLS, under the age of ten

Women's Minyan was first performed by Israel's National Theater, Habimah, at the Rovina Theater, directed by Noya Lancet, on July 4, 2002. It was directed by Noya Lancet, Miriam Yachil-Wax was the consulting dramaturge; it was designed by Frida Klapholtz-Avrahami. The American premiere was October 15, 2005, at the Reynolds Theater, Duke University, produced by Theater Or and Streetsigns Center for Literature and Performance.

ORIGINAL CAST, HABIMAH, JULY 2002.

CHANA SHEINHOFF	Davit Gavish
SHAINE RUTH	Tal Tsidkony
BLUMA	Inbal Shoham
GOLDIE SHEINHOFF	Liat Goren
ADINA SHEINHOFF	Lilach Caspi
FRUME KASHMAN	Dina Doronne
GITTE LEAH KASHMAN	Orna Rothberg
ETA LEIBOWITZ	Ruti Landau
TOVAH KLEIN	Revital Snir
ZEHAVA TOLEDANO	Dafna Armony
VOICE OVER NARRATION	Dov Reiser

Author's Notes on the Characters

NOTE ABOUT CLOTHING: The following are brief descriptions, not meant to be inclusive. The designer should read the rules of modest dress which open the play, and should study photographs of women in *haredi* neighborhoods to get a true feel for the dress code.

CHANA SHEINHOFF, (born Kashman) 43, mother of twelve. Imposing, queen-like, exuding a nun-like serenity and a fierce determination. Dressed simply but attractively, with a headscarf that covers all her hair.

SHAINE RUTH, 17, CHANA's second eldest daughter. A pretty blonde girl with carefully braided, long hair. She is dressed in a plain, ankle-length jumper of a solid dark color with a high-necked, long-sleeved shirt, or an equally plain, modest blouse and long skirt, also of solid color.

BLUMA, 19, CHANA's eldest daughter. Slim and pretty, she wears clothes that seem matronly, and her carefully coifed wig proclaims her status as a married woman.

GOLDIE SHEINHOFF, 69, CHANA's mother-in-law, highly respected widow of a great Torah scholar. Stooped, with a gray wig, she exudes great moral power and authority.

ADINA SHEINHOFF, 33, CHANA's sister-in-law, and GOLDIE SHEINHOFF's only daughter. ADINA is fragile, shy, like a wounded sparrow, belying her fierce intelligence. She has a slight stutter. She is dressed in clothes that hide her attractive figure completely. Her hair is cut short in a no-nonsense style and left completely uncovered to show her unmarried status, a stigma at her age.

FRUME KASHMAN, 63, CHANA's mother. A harsh, angular woman, she wears a severe version of the traditional headscarf that covers all her hair. She walks with a cane.

GITTE LEAH KASHMAN, 45, CHANA's older sister. Overweight, self-important, the wife of an ADMOR—an acronym that translated means: "our lord, our teacher, our rabbi"—an honorific assumed by members of the rabbinic community wishing to separate themselves from their less successful, or less ambitious, peers. She wears the traditional pointed turban, called a *schpitz*, to denote her status. Her clothes are modest, but flashier than the others.

ETA LEIBOWITZ, 38, CHANA's neighbor and former advisee. She is heavy, slow, with a head scarf that seems to squeeze her face and thrust it forward. She speaks with a heavy Yiddish accent.

TOVAH KLEIN, 42, CHANA's former friend. Thin, in a long shapeless dress with a head scarf, big glasses and no make-up. She is the woman's attendant at the ritual baths, *mikvah*.

ZEHAVA TOLEDANO, 40, CHANA's friend, a divorcee. A large, poor Sephardic woman, dressed in inexpensive, well-worn clothes, her hair covered with the long snood favored by Sephardic haredi women. Her clothing denotes a lower socio-economic status than the others. She is strong-minded, loyal, independent, and proud.

xiv

TWO YOUNG GIRLS, under the age of ten, who play the ghost children. They are dressed all in white—long-sleeved, high collared white dresses, white tights, white shoes.

The Place

PROLOGUE—An empty stage, ten chairs.

ACT ONE—The interior of the Sheinhoff home in Jerusalem, a living room.

INTERMISSION

ACT TWO—Same interior transformed into a magic Circle of Judgment.

EPILOGUE—The streets of ultra-Orthodox Meah Shearim in Jerusalem.

The Time

PROLOGUE—2001

ACT ONE—Morning, two years later

ACT TWO—Later the same day

EPILOGUE—Evening, the same day

Prologue

An empty stage. Down stage a row of twelve plain, high–backed, empty wooden chairs. On each rests the folded clothing of a haredi *woman or girl. One by one, the actors enter in their normal street clothes—jeans, leather jackets, low cut dresses etc. Each stands behind a chair.*

MAN'S VOICE: [*deep, authoritative and demanding.*] "In the merit of saintly women were the generation enslaved in Egypt redeemed. As in the first redemption, so will it be in the final redemption, which will come about because of the saintliness of women. Therefore *women must be* modest…and refuse to follow the temptations of fashion as practiced by the gentiles. True happiness, eternal happiness, can be found in the exercise of modesty. Because in every moment that she is dressed modestly, a woman performs a good deed according to the spirit of the Torah, bringing endless happiness and good to themselves and their families, a good that benefits the entire world. With the power of their modesty, modest women influence the rest of the women in the world, bringing down a spirit of purity and good behavior.

As the MAN'S VOICE *speaks, the* ACTORS *begin to remove their clothing (underneath are bodysuits) as if hearkening to the male directives.*

MAN'S VOICE: The laws of modesty. The laws of modest dress are not simply a matter of personal choice, but specific, detailed laws stated clearly in the Code of Jewish Law.

Modesty: a woman shall not wear man's clothing. She must not wear anything flashy or loud, like clothes with embroidery, or sequins, or big flowers in the front or back, or clothing with appliqués, wording, and so forth. Clothing that is form-fitting is absolutely forbidden, and it is simple and plain to any person with sense that this is the biggest stumbling block to modest dress. She shall wear no bright colors. Red is the color of licentiousness, and licentiousness brings sin. Denim clothing and sneakers are not fit to be worn by those seeking modesty.

The ACTORS *take the* haredi *clothing from the chair and begin to dress in accordance with the instructions read by* MAN'S VOICE. *They do this modestly, no flesh showing. If they remove trousers, it is only after they have put a skirt on top of it.*

MAN'S VOICE: The Law of Covering: the law of covering the body has as its purpose to hide the flesh from foreign eyes. Clothing made from lace or transparent in any part, does not constitute lawful covering—and this is the problem with white shirts, almost all of which are see-through, and so you must wear another garment underneath. Little girls must be educated to this from the earliest age. From the age of three, it is absolutely forbidden for them to show their bodies.

And these are the particulars of the laws: The Sleeves:

The ACTORS *finish putting on their outfits. They raise up their arms, checking the sleeves according to the text as it is read.*

MAN'S VOICE: The strict interpretation of the law requires that the arms be covered until the palm of the hand, and this is praiseworthy. However, those who wish to be lenient may permit the arm to be covered until beneath the elbow. But in any case, the elbow must be covered. And this is why one should not wear clothing with wide sleeves that might reveal the elbow—even accidentally—when the hands are raised up.

The Neck—

ACTORS *feel the sides of their necks as instructed.*

MAN'S VOICE: It is permitted to see the neck. The boundaries of the neck are: The sides—from the place where the neck descends into the shoulder—this must be covered. The front: from the collarbone and down, it must be covered. The back: from the first vertebra of the spine, it must be covered. There are those whose custom it is to wear only a buttoned-up collar. Failure to button the collar is very commonplace, and one must be on guard, paying careful attention to where the first button on a blouse is located, as well as to the width of the opening in sweaters and collarless dresses.

Stockings:

ACTORS *put on stockings.*

MAN'S VOICE: The wearing of stockings is mandatory. Our sages have written at length about the obligation to cover the leg from the knee to the bottom of the foot. And for those who observe stringently, the wearing of thin, transparent stockings does not fulfill this obligation. The wearing of transparent stockings or fishnet stockings is forbidden. One must wear stockings through which the flesh cannot be easily discerned. One should not wear knee-socks, because this might lead to revealing a place which is forbidden to reveal. Stockings with bold patterns and bright colors should not be worn by the modest, because they attract the eye. It is forbidden to go without stockings even in one's own home.

The ACTORS, *now fully dressed in ultra-Orthodox clothes, check the length of their dresses.*

MAN'S VOICE: The length of the dress. The knee must be covered in all events, whether sitting or standing. And the sages of our generation have already ruled that a dress must fall no less than ten centimeters below the knee, because if a dress falls just below the knee while standing, when one sits it is sure to ride up and reveal forbidden places. And this is a terrible sin recognized by all. And certain kinds of material which are likely to ride up even further when sitting, must be compensated for by lengthening them still further, so that the knee will not be revealed under any circumstances. It is mandatory to check how much every piece of clothing rides up when one sits down, in order to calculate the minimum length of the garment necessary to cover the knee. And those that go beyond the law and lengthen their skirts still further, this is praiseworthy.

The ACTORS *begin to cover their hair.*

MAN'S VOICE: The head. A married woman is required to cover all the hair on her head, either with a head covering or a wig, according to the custom. When is a wig permissible? When one can clearly see that it is a wig. A modest head covering is the crowning glory of a woman, wife, and mother. It is forbidden that one should mistake her wig for her own hair, but it should be clearly a foreign body on her.

CHANA *starts. She leaves her chair and goes offstage. The Actors continue their transformation, ignoring her.*

MAN'S VOICE: [*continues reading without interruption.*] It is forbidden that a wig be styled in a disheveled manner, because the act of wearing disheveled hair is a sin, an imitation of the whoring ways of the dregs of humanity. And this is true also of all types of wigs styled in a way that is eye-catching or strange. Because, after all, the whole reason for hair covering is to discourage strangers from catching the eyes of strangers. And women must be vigilant in overseeing the quiet, modest style and length of their wigs.

The ACTORS *transformation into* haredi *women in* haredi *dress is complete.*

CHANA: [*off. Screaming*] ENOUGH!!

A door slams. A male voice shouts angrily: "Chana!" The ACTORS *freeze, looking up. Beat.* CHANA *reenters, fleeing. Her head covering is half off. Her face and neck are stained with red marks. She tries to run through the row of chairs. She trips on her own empty chair and falls.* SHAINE RUTH *and* BLUMA *rush to help her up.* BLUMA *touches* CHANA's *bleeding cheek, looks in horror at her own hand, now tainted with her mother's blood.* SHAINE RUTH *grabs her mother's arm.* CHANA *breaks free. Like a frightened, trapped animal, she looks for escape, and heads toward the door at stage right.* FRUME *grabs her arm.*

FRUME: If you leave now, you will regret it until the end of your days!

CHANA *shakes off her mother's restraining arm. Running, she circles the stage once, then disappears.* SHAINE RUTH, BLUMA *and* FRUME *return to their places in the row, and together with the rest, retreat with the chairs and disappear into the darkness.*

MAN'S VOICE: Compiled, with the grace of God, by Talmud scholars, under the supervision and guidance of the Gaonim, Rav Shalom Elyashiv, *Shlita*, Rav Shlomo Zalman Auerbach, *Shlita*, Rav Ben Tziyon Aba Shaul, *Shlita*, Rav Shmuel HaLevi Vanzer, *Shlita*, Rav Sheinberg, *Shlita*, Rav Nissim Karlitz, *Shlita*. Rav Zilbershtein, *Shlita*, Rav Luria, *Shlita*....

Black.

Act 1

Scene one

The living/dining room in an ultra-Orthodox Jewish home in a Jerusalem apartment building. The room is worn, but very clean. Large bookcases filled with Bibles, heavy Talmudic volumes, and ritual objects line the walls: Sabbath candlesticks, a silver menorah, wine cups, spice boxes, a citron holder. Pictures of revered, bearded rabbis peer down from the walls. Stage right, the front door. Stage left, a back entrance. Along the back wall, to the right and left of the window, there's one exit to the other rooms and another to the kitchen.

The furniture includes a large dining room table which, when lit to effect, resembles an altar. There are chairs and a telephone stand. Children's toys are scattered over the floor and table. There is an empty baby stroller, a laundry basket filled with clean laundry, an ironing board. A room left hurriedly. Upstage center, a large window between the bookcases dominates the room, bringing in the outside world. Like an all seeing-eye, the unseen but powerful male presence outside intrudes constantly through the window. Alternatively, actors may look towards the audience through an imagined window.

9

Off, a MALE VOICE *reads Psalm 75, and a* CHORUS OF MEN *repeat after him, line by line, in a crescendo of threatening sound. Individual calls of "Pritza" (whore) and "Cherem" (excommunication) ring out.*

SHAINE RUTH *enters from the right. She surveys the disorder with dismay. Off, a* CHORUS OF MEN *shout: "A shame and a disgrace! It's shameful, it's wantonness."*

SHAINE RUTH *hurries to look out the window. She is visibly horrified and confused. She turns her back on it, picking up the laundry basket. Enter* BLUMA *from the back entrance.*

SHAINE RUTH: [*throwing laundry basket aside.*] Bluma! I'm so glad you've come!

BLUMA: I had to go all the way around. It's just not modest for…a woman to press her body through such a crowd of men.

SHAINE RUTH: [*wiping away tears.*] I thought you'd forgotten.

BLUMA: How could I forget?! Granny Fruma called me twice yesterday, and Rav (Rabbi) Aaron even reminded my husband—

SHAINE RUTH: So what took you so long?

BLUMA: [*evasively.*] I'm sorry, I was feeling—[*beat.*] not well.

SHAINE RUTH: Never mind. Thank God you're here now. [*indicating the window*]. Just listen to what they're saying about her! Oh, I wish this was over already!

They embrace, listening to the threatening male voices filtering in through the window. Pause.

BLUMA: Maybe she won't come. I don't believe even she'd have the *chutzpah* to face all those men.

SHAINE RUTH: But what if she does? What if she brings the police? Oh, let's get out of here, now!

BLUMA: You know it's forbidden. We've been told what we have to do. [*suddenly taking in the disorder.*] Shaine Ruth! How did you leave everything in such a mess?

SHAINE RUTH: I ran after Shimmy with his *tzitzis* [*holds them in her hand.*]

BLUMA: [*appalled.*] *How* could you forget such a thing?

SHAINE RUTH: [*hurt, defensive.*] I dressed all the little ones myself. It's the one thing I forgot.

BLUMA: [*beginning to straighten up.*] You poor thing! When I was here they knew they'd better behave themselves. Come on, let's clean this mess up!

SHAINE RUTH: [*with one ear cocked to the window, she picks up a holy book from the table.*] Since you got married, everything is so much harder!

BLUMA: You're seventeen already, Shaine Ruth. You should be able to manage. Make the children do their share.

SHAINE RUTH: They try. But they are still so young. And so am I. I don't know how to be a mother to ten children.

Off. VOICES *call out:* "Shun her! We won't allow it! In the name of the Torah!" SHAINE RUTH *drops the books and runs to the window.*

BLUMA: What are you doing, Shaine Ruth! Get away from that window. Come, finish with these books.

SHAINE RUTH: [*still peering out of the window, agitated.*] *Oy* no! The older boys are still here in the yard!

BLUMA: It can't be!

SHAINE RUTH: Yes! Yitzchak and Eliahu! They're standing there with the rest of the men! [*guilty and appalled.*] *Oy va'a voy!!* Are they also going to scream insults at *Ima* (Mother)?

BLUMA: [*taking out her frustrations on the cleaning.*] She's brought it all on herself!

SHAINE RUTH: What's gotten into you? Honor thy father and mother. It's the fifth commandment. [*looking out the window, suddenly relaxing. She waves, sighs.*] That's it. They're gone. Granny Frume just came back and took them. [*Pause.*] Let's also run away, you and I! *Ima* will come and the place will be empty.

BLUMA: I already told you. It's forbidden. Someone has to be here to get rid of her.

SHAINE RUTH: Why? If she doesn't find anyone…?

BLUMA: Rav Aaron said.

SHAINE RUTH: But why us? Why not Granny or Father?

BLUMA: Shaine Ruth!! Who are we to question the words of the holy Rav?

SHAINE RUTH: All right, all right! [*noises off bring back their attention to the window.*] Look Bluma! More men are coming! Instead of spending their precious time learning the Torah, they're here "protecting" us from her. It's sinful.

BLUMA: [*arranging things, furious.*] Another mark on her black soul.

SHAINE RUTH: Oy! Bluma come look! They've brought clubs. [*frightened.*] You don't think…you don't think they'll beat her up, do you? What a horror!

BLUMA: What a *mitzvah!* [good deed].

SHAINE RUTH: How can you say that?!! These are not *your* words, Bluma. [*staring out the window longingly.*] I wonder how she looks now.

BLUMA: I couldn't care less. Come back here—stop staring and put away this laundry.

SHAINE RUTH: [*lost in thought.*] Two years. Two whole years since she left. Such a long time. I've tried so hard to forget, the way everyone told us, but I just can't. Last night, I dreamt about her. She was braiding my hair and—[*noise off draws her to window.*] Oh, look! It's him!

BLUMA: Who?

SHAINE RUTH: Your…. [*changes her mind, lies.*] No. Nothing. I just thought…

BLUMA: *Please* get away from that window. Do you want the entire neighborhood to see you?

The room is in order, except for the table. BLUMA *takes off the tablecloth and hands it to* SHAINE RUTH.

Go bring an ironed one. And fix your braid. We don't want her to think that without her we're falling apart at the seams.

SHAINE RUTH *looks toward her sister, toward the window. She hesitates a moment, then exits.* VOICES *off:* "Excommunication! Never! Jezebel!"

BLUMA: [*to herself.*] She won't come. She won't have the *chutzpah* to stand up against all of them. Even she couldn't be that shameless.

SHAINE RUTH *returns with a tablecloth. She again glances toward the window, toward her sister. She begins to speak, thinks better of it, and remains silent. Facing each other on either side of the long table, they grasp the tablecloth and with a single movement let it drop over the table, which acquires the aura of ritual.*

BLUMA: [*smiling ironically.*] Shaine Ruth! You call this ironed?

SHAINE RUTH: [*laughingly, in sad agreement.*] Nothing is the same as it was when *Ima* was here. She used to spend an hour ironing the Sabbath tablecloth until it was perfect. With her, everything was clean and shining and polished….Remember?

BLUMA: [*hardening.*] What I remember is that she ruined my chances for the marriage I dreamed about.

Pause.

SHAINE RUTH: I saw him just now. He was out there, with the others.

BLUMA: [*agitated.*] Joseph Graetz? [*she takes a step toward the window, then stops in pain.*] It was her fault! Everything was her fault. She destroyed any chance I had with a man like him. And now she's coming back to destroy your chances. All of a sudden she loves her children so much. All of a sudden she misses us so much....

SHAINE RUTH: I miss her also. [*beat.*] So much.

BLUMA: What a little fool you are, Shaine Ruth! Get this into your head once and for all: the fewer people who see her, the better your chances are for a decent match. Just imagine the mothers of all the yeshiva boys in Meah Shearim looking out the window as she marches to our door with the police.... Do you think any one of them would agree to be your mother-in-law after that?

Off. SOUND OF POLICE SIREN.

There, you see!? That's your precious mother. She's brought the Cossacks from the police!

SHAINE RUTH: [*frightened.*] Oh, no! I can't face her!

BLUMA: Why should *you* be ashamed to face *her*? *She* is the one who ruined our family's honor, poured filth over our good name. *She* is the one who abandoned a husband and twelve children and went to live with a woman! [SHAINE RUTH *is shocked.*] Yes, to live with her, like husband and wife! Why can't *you* face *her*?!

SHAINE RUTH: Because of all the lies we told to the children, to the Rabbis during the divorce trial!

BLUMA: [*stubbornly.*] Everything we said at the trial was true!

SHAINE RUTH: That she was a terrible mother, that we didn't love her, that she didn't keep a kosher kitchen?! Don't you even remember that, once, she was the most wonderful mother in the world?

15

BLUMA: [*bitterly.*] No. That's not what I remember.

SHANIE RUTH: [*grabbing her sister's shoulders.*] She knew we were lying then. And she'll know it now. You know it's impossible to lie to *Ima*.

BLUMA: [*shaken, suddenly frightened and guilty.*] We only did what they told us to do, Rav Aaron, Father…Granny. They said sometimes a lie can be a good deed, like the lie Jacob told to Isaac to get his blessing.

Sharp knocks on the door.

SHAINE RUTH: It's her! She's here! Are you going to open the door?

BLUMA: [*helplessly.*] If she'd only just disappear! If the earth would just open up and swallow her, like it did to Korach!

SHAINE RUTH: [*running to the door and opening it.*] *Ima?*

Scene two

The main door opens. A head sticks in. It's ETA. *After her, another head intrudes:* TOVAH.

TOVAH: Why are you pushing me?

ETA: I'm not; I'm just faster.

TOVAH: *Er iz, zayt mir moykhl, a mentsh.* (*i.e.* "Her entire personality says please forgive me.")

ETA: *Keyner zet nisht zayn eygenem hoyker* (i.e. "We are blind to our own defects.")

SHAINE RUTH: [relieved and let down.] Oh, it's you. Shalom.

TOVAH: [*with false sweetness.*] Shaine Ruth, sweetheart.

I'm so sorry to bother you. Perhaps, maybe, you have a little cooking oil Eta could borrow?

ETA: I was just in the middle of making a compote…

TOVAH: [*elbowing her out of the way.*] What compote?

ETA: Let me explain. I'm already explaining!

TOVAH: You're all mixed up. I'll explain.

ETA: I got mixed up because you're interrupting me. [*to* SHAINE RUTH] Eta was in the middle of the compote—

TOVAH: The potato kugel.

ETA: Yes, right, when suddenly I realized I was running out of vinegar…[*to* TOVAH.] Why are you pinching me?

SHAINE RUTH: Vinegar for potato kugel?

BLUMA: Maybe tell us already what it is you want?

TOVAH: Oil.

ETA: Right. That's what I wanted to say!

SHAINE RUTH: I'll go see. [*she turns to go.*]

BLUMA: [*stopping her.*] There's no need. We're also out of vinegar.

SHAINE RUTH: [*laughing and whispering.*] Oil.

BLUMA: We're out of that too.

ETA: How do you know? You don't even live here anymore. [*turning with an ingratiating smile to* SHAINE RUTH] Shaine-leh…

BLUMA: [*cutting her short.*] Why don't you try the Goldbergs?

ETA: No one answers the door over there.

SHAINE RUTH: (*whispering to* BLUMA.) Because everyone is too busy looking out of their windows...

ETA: Right.

TOVAH: Right what?

ETA: Right this minute I wanted to go down to Weis in the grocery. My husband, Shlomo, God bless him, loves potato kugel so much—but it's impossible to get out of the building because of all the men hanging around outside. Could it be, maybe, you might have an idea, why?

SHAINE RUTH: They were sent by the Rabbi, Rav—

BLUMA: [*silencing her.*] Please, excuse us. [*as in "excuse me, I've got to get going..."*] We're waiting for our Granny....

SHAINE RUTH: [catching on.]—and we haven't finished straightening up yet. So if you'll excuse us....

TOVAH: We can help you with something, maybe? [*she picks something off the floor, her eyes roaming for new opportunities.*]

BLUMA: There's no need, really. Thank you. [BLUMA *takes the object out of* TOVAH's *hand and finds a place for it.*]

ETA: It must be so hard for you without your Mother.

TOVAH: [*pretending to be casual, but intensely interested.*] How is she, by the way? Have you heard from her?

No answer. TOVAH *clucks her tongue.* ETA *shakes her head.*

ETA: Outside they are saying—

BLUMA: We don't listen to gossip.

TOVAH: Very good! It's a terrible sin to listen to loose tongues.

ETA: Just because all Meah Shearim is talking about her, doesn't mean a thing.

TOVAH: By me in my ritual baths, I never allow idle gossip.

ETA: God forbid! But maybe its best for them to be prepared, *farshteyst* (understand)?

TOVAH: I, for one, do not believe that Chana is going to come here dressed like a slut—

SHAINE RUTH: What!!!

TOVAH:—even though it wouldn't be the first time. She's already been seen that way.

SHAINE RUTH: By whom?!

TOVAH: People.

SHAINE RUTH: When?

ETA: She's been seen. Walking around in a red mini skirt—and cleavage between her toes in open sandals.

TOVAH:—with her hair uncovered.

ETA:—on Ben Yehuda Street.

Pause.

SHAINE RUTH: [*shocked.*] Who told you such a thing?

TOVAH: [*with the pretense of sorrow.*] Rebbitzen Fishbein.

SHAINE RUTH: And you believe her? You, who had to get mother's approval on what kind of knot to make in your headscarf? You asked her advice on everything.

TOVAH: What do you want from me? It's not me who's spreading these stories.

BLUMA: [*aside, sarcastically.*] Of course not.

TOVAH: [*indicating* ETA.] She said her husband heard it from Rav Aaron himself!

SHAINE RUTH: That just can't be.... We know our mother....

21

BLUMA: She wouldn't dare come here dressed like that!

SHAINE RUTH: What? You believe them? That mother, our mother, paraded herself down the street dressed like they say?!

BLUMA *doesn't answer.*

TOVAH: [*triumphant.*] If Rebbitzen Fishbein told Rebbitzen Klein, who is Rivkeleh's—Eta's daughter's—Torah teacher, that her husband, Rav Fishbein, heard it in *synagogue* from a yeshiva boy who is very close to Rav Aaron himself, and he heard it from the assistant beadle who saw her with his own eyes walking down Ben Yehuda street in a red mini skirt, then who are we to doubt it?!

SHAINE RUTH: The assistant beadle told it to Rebbitzen Fishbein?

TOVAH: To the yeshiva boy.

ETA: His friend...

SHAINE RUTH: The yeshiva boy told it to Rebbitzen Fishbein?

TOVAH: To the Rav.

ETA: Fishbein.

TOVAH: Right.

ETA: What's right?

TOVAH: That's right,—

SHAINE RUTH: [*interrupting.*] No! None of it's right. It's all wrong, all lies, stories, idle gossip. [*to* BLUMA.] Don't you remember how strict *Ima* was with us? How she checked that our elbows

22

were always covered, and our blouses buttoned up to our chins? It just can't be!

BLUMA: It can't be? They are telling you that it came from Rav Aaron himself! Would you accuse Moses of lying? Eliahu the Prophet of lying? We are just women. There are things we can't understand. We're just not on their level.

ETA: Wise like her mother.

TOVAH: [*to* BLUMA, *commiserating.*] What *mazal* that he stopped her from coming to your wedding.

BLUMA: [*angry.*] Mrs. Klein!!

ETA: After she ruined your match with—[*indicating window.*]

BLUMA: How do you know about that?!

SHAINE RUTH: [*surprised.*] *Ima* wanted to come to your wedding? But Rav Aaron and Father told us that she didn't want to see us!

BLUMA: [*glowering angrily at* TOVAH, *to* SHAINE RUTH.] What she wanted was to ruin it, Shaine Ruth. What she wanted was to put on her festive wig and dance at my wedding like nothing happened.

ETA: [*to* SHAINE RUTH.] So Rav Aaron advised your father to take out a restraining order against her, *farshteyst?*

BLUMA: Mrs. Klein! The wise know what they say; fools say what they know.

SHAINE RUTH: [*confused, broken.*] So she *did* want to come to your wedding...

ETA: *Avaadah* (of course).

SHAINE RUTH: She wanted to see us...

Outside the men's VOICES *call out threateningly: "Pritza! Cherem! Nedui!* (Whore! Banish her! Shun her!). *The women listen, intimidated.*

TOVAH: What a racket those men make! You should close the windows. It will frighten the children.

The girls become visibly tense. Pause.

TOVAH: [*noticing their discomfort.*] Where are the children?

ETA: Shimmy wasn't in kindergarten with my Yaakov this morning. Is he sick?

Without waiting for an invitation, ETA *and* TOVAH *exit to search through the rooms.* BLUMA *and* SHAINE RUTH *hold a consultation.*

BLUMA: Don't say a word about the children! Unless you want all Meah Shearim to know!

SHAINE RUTH: [*nods her agreement, in a whispered complaint.*] Why didn't you tell me about the wedding?

BLUMA: Rav Aaron said it would be better for you not to know....

They exit, in search of the neighbors.

Scene three

FRUME: [*off.*] Shaineleh, there's a reason you left the door open?

> *Enter* FRUME *from the back door, smiling. Dragging tiredly behind her is* GITTE LEAH, *heavy and ill-humored.*

SHAINE RUTH: [*running to* FRUME.] *Granny.* It's so good you're here!

FRUME: What did you think? That I'd leave you here on your own? Come bring a chair for your Auntie, Shaineleh. She came specially all the way from B'nai Brak [*warmly.*] Gitte Leah: Come. Sit. Rest. You deserve it.

> SHAINE RUTH *brings a chair for* GITTE LEAH, *then goes into the kitchen.*

GITTE LEAH: Good *maideleh.* I'm fainting from hunger, and my back is killing me.

BLUMA: [*comes in and runs to* FRUME.] Granny!

FRUME: Bluma-leh! How pale you look! You stopped eating?

BLUMA: [*embarrassed, eager to change the subject.*] I'm fine, really, God be blessed. [*whisper.*] Granny, where are the children?

FRUME: This is not for you to worry about, my sweet granddaughter. Everything is arranged as it should be. Such a relief! If she has the nerve to show up now, we'll show her a thing or two!

In the middle of FRUME'S *speech, enter* GOLDIE SHEINHOFF.

SHEINHOFF, WITH HER DAUGHTER, ADINA: [*sitting. To herself.*] Poor children! It's so terrible!

FRUME: [*surprised.*] What's so terrible? To save your son's children from more damage and pain?

ETA and TOVAH *peek into the room, eager for the latest gossip.*

SHAINE RUTH: [*noticing them. Warningly.*]—Granny...

SHEINHOFF: [*to* FRUME.] God watch over us! Aren't they Chana's children also? Your own daughter's children? Don't you have any pity for her at all?

FRUME: No! I'm ashamed to be her mother.

SHEINHOFF God help us!

GITTE LEAH: If God had seen fit to bless me with twelve children instead of her...

FRUME: Say a blessing for the three you do have, Gitte. Your health is so delicate.

SHAINE RUTH: [*more forcefully.*] Granny...

GITTE LEAH: What is it already Shaine Ruth? [*discovering the intruding* ETA *and* TOVAH. *Warningly.*] Oh, Mother, we have visitors.

FRUME *turns and sees* ETA *and* TOVAH.

ETA: [*jumping out first.*] We came to borrow a little—? [*looks enquiringly at* TOVAH.]

TOVAH: Excuse me Eta. Let me.... Eta was just in the middle of making a potato kugel when she ran out of—

ETA: Oil?

TOVAH: [*relieved.*] Right.

ETA: As it is written: Better fine oil than a fine neighbor...

TOVAH: The opposite! "Better a fine neighb—"

FRUME: [*interrupting.*] So, in the children's bedrooms you were drilling for oil?

TOVAH: We made a wrong turn.

FRUME: Take our fine guests to the kitchen, girls, and *find* them anything they need. [*to herself.*] So they can *find* their way out! [*out loud.*] Don't you see they are in a terrible rush to go home?

The four walk toward the kitchen, ETA *and* TOVAH *dragging reluctantly behind the girls, pausing for greetings. They are overwhelmed at meeting the important Rabbi's widow and his daughter.*

TOVAH: Shalom, Rebbitzen Sheinhoff.

ETA: Shalom Adina.

27

BLUMA *and* SHAINE RUTH *hurry them off.*

FRUME: *Yenta-kvetches!* (gossiping complainers). They came to sniff out the latest gossip!

GITTE LEAH: Tovah will soon go running off to announce it in the ritual baths, and Eta, that Red Heifer, will share it with every neighbor in the building.

FRUME: We have to get rid of them before *she* shows up!

SHEINHOFF: My poor grandchildren. The twins cried all the way. Malka had to carry them, in turns. She's just a child herself.

FRUME: [*whispering.*] Sssssh. It's all their mother's fault!

During this dialogue, ETA *and* TOVAH *reenter carrying a large bottle of oil, which they will drag around with them from now on.* SHAINE RUTH *and* BLUMA *follow.*

ADINA: [*with a slight stutter, apologetically.*] Excuse me but…but not to let her see her children two whole years…? How can this be right? How can it be just?

GITTE LEAH: As my husband the scholar says—"the belly of the wicked shall suffer want."

SHEINHOFF: We didn't have a choice, Adina. Her children were suffering. Until we were finally able to restore a little order in the house—[*painfully, delicately, yet with a touch of criticism.*] When you'll have children of your own, you'll understand.

GITTE LEAH: [*cruelly.*] After we merit to rejoice with you under the marriage canopy, with God's help!

Disturbance. TOVAH *manages to brush by a pile of books and sends them flying. She hurries to pick them up and arrange them.*

FRUME: [*examining arrangement of books.*] What's this, Mrs. Klein? The Code of Jewish Law on top of the Bible? This is a God-fearing house!

TOVAH: Of course. I knew that... [*hurriedly rearranges them.*]

GITTE LEAH: Everything has to be in its place. The holiest on top, the less holy beneath it. Whoever doesn't understand that, will wind up on the bottom, in hell!

TOVAH: God protect us!

FRUME: I see that you've struck oil, so...

They look at each other in confusion, whispering, consulting, pushing each other in different directions. They pick up the bottle of oil.

TOVAH: Yes.

ETA: No.

TOVAH: [*probing.*] So, the children are all right?

ETA: Where are they?

TOVAH: I didn't know what to think this morning when Shimmy didn't go to school with her Yaakov....

GITTE LEAH: Excuse me, but this is a family matter.

TOVAH: We're all one big family here.

ETA: Not like you over there in B'nai Brak.

TOVAH: [*offended.*] We saw they're not here!

GITTE LEAH: This is private!

ETA: [*incredulous.*] Private? In Meah Shearim?

[*She laughs, indicating the window. To* FRUME, *confidentially.*] Outside, they are saying she's bringing the television.

FRUME: The television!? [to SHEINHOFF.] And you want me to feel sorry for her!

The universal horror over the possibility of television film crews turning up, unifies the women to the extent that even TOVAH *and* ETA *are allowed to join in.*

SHAINE RUTH: Granny, what are we going to do?!

FRUME: I must call Rav Aaron at once!

FRUME *marches to the telephone, and the group parades behind her.*

BLUMA: Yes! Call him, Granny. Rav Aaron will tell us what to do.

SHEINHOFF: She's calling Rav Aaron? I also want to hear.... [*moves in closer to phone.*]

TOVAH: [*aside.*] Oh God—watch over us.... Eta! Why didn't you tell me that they were going to put me on the television? Come, let's go....

ETA: [*righteously.*] We're not going anywhere! You yourself said we were one big family...This involves all of Meah Shearim, every

God-fearing woman in Israel.... [*she fixes her wig. Whispers.*] How do I look?

TOVAH: [*with irony.*] Like the Rose of Sharon....

FRUME: Shhh! [*into phone.*] Hello? Rav Aaron? Shalom, shalom. Yes, it's Frume Kashman speaking. Yes, Rav. Yes, we did exactly what you told us. Yes, your boys are here outside chanting Psalms. But Rav Aaron, what if she brings the *pork-eaters* from the television? [*listens.*] May God bless you, and every blessing to your wife, the Rebbitzen. [*she hangs up.*]

GITTE LEAH: What did he say?

FRUME: He said [*she pauses, striking a saintly pose, palms together, pointing upward.*] that if she only tries, this time they'll break also her arms and legs.

SHAINE RUTH: [*appalled, whispers to* BLUMA.] We have to warn her....

BLUMA: Keep out of it.

SHEINHOFF: [*emotionally.*] *It's forbidden for them to* touch her! You hear? To harm a hair on my Chanaleh's head!

FRUME: Tell it to Rav Aaron. He's your relative.

SHEINHOFF *attempts to go back to the phone but hasn't the strength.* ADINA *catches her before she falls, helping her back into her chair.*

FRUME: [*to* BLUMA *and* SHAINE RUTH.] Go. Bring your *Savta* a cup of mint tea.

The girls exit. FRUME *goes to* SHEINHOFF.

FRUME: I tell you—and don't think it's not hard for me to say this, I'm her mother after all—she's brought this all on herself! She saw the pit in front of her and jumped in with both feet. Would she listen to reason? Did she take pity on the little ones? Why should *I* pity her now?

SHEINHOFF: [*to* FRUME.] What's the matter with you? [*to the others.*] With all of you? Have you forgotten everything? [*she leans on* ADINA.]

ADINA: Please Mother, don't excite yourself.

SHEINHOFF: Have you forgotten—who Chanaleh was? [*to* ETA *and* TOVAH.] How all the Rabbis in Meah Shearim sent women to her for counseling? How you yourselves wouldn't put one foot in front of the other without hearing her opinion? [*she rises, walking around the dining room table, as if willing the past to come back.*] Have you forgotten Chana's Sabbath table? [*remembering with joy.*] How everything shone! The children, all twelve of them, smiling, clean from their baths. The boys in their ironed starched white shirts, the girls in their pretty dresses....and Chana, like a queen. [*goes to the head of the table, touches the chair.*] And my son, my Yankele, a king at the head...[*covers her face and weeps.*] Have we no pity for Chanaleh? She was the joy of my life!

In the middle of the monologue, SHAINE RUTH *enters with the tea. She pauses, listening. When* SHEINHOFF *finishes, the sound of a police siren and then a megaphone is heard from outside: "Stand back. Don't block the way!"* SHAINE RUTH *drops the cup.*

GITTE LEAH: I told you! She's bringing the Cossacks!

SHEINHOFF *grows faint.*

ADINA: Mother, are you all right?

SHEINHOFF: [*shakes head "no."*] Take me to the kitchen Adinaleh. I don't want to be here.

ADINA: Come Mother, come. I'll make you another cup.

Harsh knocks on the door.

MAN'S VOICE: Police! Open up!

GITTE LEAH: What a disgrace!

SHAINE RUTH: [*to* BLUMA.] I can't face her. I can't!

BLUMA: Calm down!

ETA: [*to* TOVAH, *whispering in delight.*] In a minute, there's going to be a huge scandal....

TOVAH: [*warningly.*] *Oy-va-Voy* if your husband finds out you were with her....

ETA: [*threateningly.*] As it is written: "Who tells his friend's secret sheds blood." *Farshteyst?*

TOVAH: *Ah- vaadah!*

> TOVAH *and* ETA *prepare themselves for the* TV *cameras. Another knock on the door.*

MAN'S VOICE: Police! Open up!

FRUME: Gitte Leah, go open!

GITTE LEAH: I can't. I'm *plotzing* (collapsing). My back....

Pause. No one moves.

FRUME: [*in a trembling voice, without moving from her place.*] What are you all so terrified of? Outside, the police helped her. But here, inside, no one will help her. Bluma-leh, go open the door....

BLUMA *approaches the door. Stops. Backtracks.*

Scene four

The front door opens. Enter CHANA, *carrying a purse and a shopping bag.*

CHANA: [*to the police behind her.*] Thank you, officer. I'll be all right now. There's no need for you to come in.

An extended pause: They have not seen each other for two years—her daughters, family, friends. They examine each other. The moment bristles with tension.

CHANA: Bluma-leh, a married woman [*approaches* BLUMA.]

BLUMA, *who has stood frozen opposite her at a safe distance, instinctively moves back. Pause. She turns her back on her mother, and moves away.*

CHANA: [*painfully.*] Shaine-leh?

SHAINE RUTH *draws closer. They hug each other wordlessly, intensely.* CHANA, *who has dreamed of this reunion for two years—holds her and caresses her. The* WOMEN *are moved despite themselves.* FRUME, *trapped by circumstances, is furious.*

FRUME: [*vindictive, every word a dagger.*] So, this is what you think? That a hug will erase what you did to them? To all of us? Suddenly, she remembers her children! You abandon twelve angels and a saintly husband and imagine you won't have to pay? One hug and everything will be fine again, what? How do you even have the *chutzpah* to walk in here—and with the Cossacks yet! Until now you at least respected the Rabbinical court order and left us in peace, but now even the Rabbis you mock! Get out of here, go! You'll pay for everything you did; and pay and pay and pay and pay, until the end of time!

With every bitter word, CHANA'S *embrace around her daughter loosens. It is as if* FRUME *is physically tearing them apart.* CHANA *will not be drawn into confrontation. She burns to see her children. She turns toward the children's bedrooms.* FRUME *blocks her way.*

CHANA: [*restrained.*] Please, let me through. [FRUME *doesn't move.*] This is *my* house. These are *my* children. I want to see them. [*to daughters.*] You did well, girls, to leave the little ones in their rooms. My wise girls. Children shouldn't have to see grownups behave like fools. [*she maneuvers around* FRUME, *continues to the bedrooms, softly calling out her children's names.*] Ruchele, Faigele, your mother is home! Shifraleh, I brought you a baby doll—come see! Moishe! Shimmy! Eliahu! My boys. There are presents for you too. Your *Ima* is back. Malka-leh, where are you? [*going from room to room.*] Are you playing hide and seek with me? [*she runs to the kitchen, encountering* SHEINHOFF *and* ADINA.] Mameh Goldie! You're here too. Adina! [*she smoothes back a stray lock of* ADINA'S *hair.*] You are still not—? [ADINA *indicates "no." A moment of shared sympathy.*] Are the children with you? [CHANA *returns to the living room, to the women.*] Where are they? [*no answer. With concern.*] Bluma, Shaine Ruth, where are the children? [*no one answers. She looks in panic from face to face around the room, as the truth begins to dawn on her. To* FRUME.] What have you done with my children?

SHAINE RUTH *walks forward.* BLUMA *holds her back.* SHEIN-HOFF *enters with* ADINA, *sighing heavily.*

CHANA: [*near panic.*] Something happened to them?

ADINA: God forbid! They are all alive and well, Chana. They're fine. [*to* SHEINHOFF.] Don't get upset, Mother. You know you're not allowed.

CHANA: [*to* FRUME.] What have you done with them!? [FRUME *turns her back. Pleading.*] Tovah, do you have my children? [TOVAH *shakes her head no.*] ETA? [*no answer.*] Have you swallowed your tongue?

TOVAH: Her husband threatened to divorce her if she talked to you.

ETA: And in the ritual baths, the women wouldn't let Tovah touch them anymore.

TOVAH: They suspected me too of being unnatural, because I was your friend.

ETA: You have no idea how *we've* suffered, because of you.

CHANA: So you have my children?

ETA: No, I don't!

TOVAH: Leave the children in peace, Chana. You need help. You're not well.

CHANA: [*restrained fury.*] When you went into depression after your fourth child, was that the advice I gave you? Or did I come to your house, day after day, bathe your kids, take you shopping, cook your meals until you were back on your feet? (TOVAH turns away, ashamed)

ETA: You helped everyone, Chana. But now the best thing you can do is leave. Remember what you told me when I came to talk to you about my Gershon? You said, "Don't force things. The damage you do to a child's tender soul can never be undone."

TOVAH: Let the children get on with their lives, Chana. Enough you've humiliated them!

CHANA: [*pleading.*] I just want to talk to them.

> TOVAH *wavers.* FRUME *gives her a withering look that says: Are you with us or against us?*

TOVAH: [*to* CHANA.] If only you had listened to me two years ago and committed yourself for treatment. Your soul is sick.... You need help.

GITTE LEAH: She isn't sick. She's corrupt....

SHAINE RUTH: Why do you have to insult her?

ETA: [*to* GITTE LEAH.] The child is right! God watch over us, why? [*to* CHANA.] Chana, you yourself must know that the proper thing to do is for you to leave here quietly.

GITTE LEAH: There's nothing for you here, are you deaf? [*imploringly.*] Adina, Rebbitzen Sheinhoff, tell her!

ADINA: Excuse me.... But I'll talk when I have something to say.

SHEINHOFF: Chanaleh, in the name of the love that I have always had for you, I'm asking you, please, go quietly....

CHANA: [*full of pain.*] Mameh Goldie, please, where are my children?

Pause. Music: TWO GIRLS, *the ghost children, appear in the background, dressed in white.* CHANA *is startled, then understands.*

CHANA: [*devastated.*] You've hidden my children from me.

Pause.

GITTE LEAH: Finally, finally, she's woken up! Yes, the house is empty. Yes, the children are gone. And *you* are not going to be able to find them.

CHANA *receives this like a blow to her stomach. She sits down heavily, hugging herself.*

FRUME: You're in pain? You're suffering? I also suffered. [*looking at* BLUMA.] I suffered when a beautiful young girl lost the her chance to marry the best match. I suffered when everything I worked for all these years—to be respected and accepted in the community of Meah Shearim—was destroyed. I suffered when I heard people say that our family wasn't worthy to marry into a Rabbinical family like the Sheinhoffs. I suffered when I watched my grandchildren crying themselves to sleep every night because they missed their mother! I warned you, Chana—I begged you—not to leave. If you'd only listened to me we could have settled everything! But you ran away. You always did exactly what was good for you.

CHANA: [*in pain.*] They cried? My poor babies.... If only I could have stayed.... But I had no choice.

FRUME: You had no choice? So now also you have no choice. Go!

GITTE LEAH: With the Cossacks, or without the Cossacks, you will never get your children back. You are a Jezebel.

TOVAH: [*drawing closer.*] Go, go, Chana, for your own good.

ETA: [*drawing closer, fearfully.*] Go, before all of Meah Shearim sees you.

TOVAH: Think about Shaine Ruth, and *her* chances for a good match! Do you want to do to her what you did to her sister? Who will want to marry the daughter of a woman who behaves like you?

SHEINHOFF: Let her breathe! What is this, a stoning? She hears us. She understands by herself. She won't hurt her children, isn't that true, Chanaleh?

CHANA: [*still in shock. To herself.*] A match for Shaine Ruth? Already?.... How time rushes by...when did I give birth to these children? When did I bring them up?.... Twelve children I raised, all by myself, without help from anyone. Twelve children I have....

FRUME: You had. Now they are motherless.

CHANA: [*waking up. Quietly.*] No. I am their mother. I am here for them.

FRUME: They don't want you.

CHANA: [*passionately.*] What do you know? I wasn't a mother like you. My children miss me. You yourself said so. I still feel them here, inside me. I am not budging from here until I see them. [*she sits down and holds herself, as if her body will break.*] My baby, my Shifraleh. How she must have grown.... [*to* ADINA.] She's walking, talking?

ADINA *nods.*

SHAINE RUTH: And Shimmy is already learning in *cheder*!

CHANA: Really? My little scholar. You must let me see them.

GITTE LEAH: Me, me, me! All your life, that's all you ever thought about. Yourself. You never cared what you were doing to everyone else. Your husband, your children. Us. We can't walk down the street because of you! So if you hope you'll work on our pity, you are an even bigger fool than I thought.

SHEINHOFF: How can you speak that way, Gitte Leah? What does our holy Torah teach us if not compassion and loving kindness?

Music: Children's motif. CHANA *hears it in her imagination. It strengthens her determination. Stares at* FRUME *bitterly.*

CHANA: Even as a child I knew not to expect pity. And I don't expect it now. [*taking out papers from her purse.*] Here. It's a court order.

FRUME: [*shocked.*] What?

CHANA: You have to let me see them. It's the law.

Shaking with emotion, the court order falls from her hand. SHAINE RUTH *picks it up, looking at her mother, who approves.*

SHAINE RUTH: [*reading.*] "The Court has decided to accept the recommendations of the social worker and, therefore, the Court nullifies all previous court orders forbidding visitation of Chana Sheinhoff with her minor children, and declares that the father,

Yaakov Sheinhoff, shall in no way prevent or interfere with said visits. The mother shall be allowed to visit once a week…"

ETA: Is this the law?

TOVAH: There are laws, and then there are laws, *farshteyst?*

FRUME: This is the law of the godless State. It's not our law. It's worth nothing in Meah Shearim.

SHAINE RUTH: No, Granny. It's a Rabbinical Court order.

FRUME: That can't be! [*to* CHANA.] The Rabbinical Court order forbids you to go near the children! [*grabbing the order from* SHAINE RUTH.]

CHANA: This is a new one.

FRUME: [*cutting her off. Reading the words out loud, incredulous.*] "And after a trial period, the Court will make its decision on the mother's request to remove the children from the father's custody…" What?! Out of the question. You fooled the Rabbis too. Rav Aaron warned us. [*tearing the page to pieces.*] Here, here, here is your court order.

CHANA: [*calmly taking more from her purse.*] The police have copies. I made a thousand of them. Enough for all of you to tear.

GITTE LEAH: [*sticking her face into* CHANA'*s, belligerently.*] It won't help you. [*with a malicious smile, crumpling up the paper.*] All you have in your hands is paper. Your children are in our hands. And we will never give them back to you. Never!

CHANA: [*for first time, losing control. She shakes* GITTE LEAH *violently by the shoulders, grabbing off her hair covering.*] God of the Universe! God of the Universe! God of the Universe! Give me back my children!!

GITTE LEAH: [*fighting back.*] How dare you touch me! Criminal! Oy, my back! *Meshuganah! Pritza!* Mother!

FRUME: [*rushing to help* GITTE LEAH.] My *maideleh*, my child! Leave her alone. *Vilda Chaya* (wild animal)!

Pandemonium. The others try to pull the sisters apart, but get entangled themselves. Nevertheless, this never turns into a cat-fight or a brawl.

SHAINE RUTH: [*trying to hold her mother back.*] Mother!

BLUMA: Enough. Stop! Please!

SHEINHOFF: *Oy vey iz mere*! (Oh, woe is me!) What is happening to us? Dear God. [*in a great voice.*] STOP IT, ALL OF YOU!

43

Everything stops. The women are in disarray, modest head coverings, clothes awry.

SHEINHOFF: Look at yourselves! It's a disgrace. Is this how pious women behave? [*pause.*] Attack her, slander her—that's what we did the minute she walked through the door. You've forgotten completely that she's the one who built this house with so much hard work and so much love. A Jew, even if he sins, is still a Jew. Let me speak to her.

All the women obey, getting ready to leave the room. Only GITTE LEAH, *still busy picking up her headcovering, seems ready to pounce again.*

ADINA: [*delicately blocking* GITTE LEAH'S *way, helping her re-cover her hair.*] Come, Gitte Leah, let's go to the kitchen. [GITTE LEAH *shrugs her off belligerently.*] Bluma, can you prepare some tea? Everyone is tired and thirsty. Let my mother talk to her....

FRUME: [*complaining to* SHEINHOFF.] *Narishkeit* (foolishness). There's no point.

ADINA: Come, Mrs. Kashman. Have a little tea.

SHAINE RUTH: Come, Granny, please.

FRUME *gathers* GITTE LEAH. *Everyone exits except* CHANA *and* SHEINHOFF.

SHEINHOFF: [*in affection and pain.*] Chana, I can't believe this is you—!

CHANA: That was nothing. Just the roar of a mother lion. But if you keep me away from my children even one more day, I will do much more than roar, I promise you that!

SHEINHOFF: Chanaleh, Chanaleh…. Isn't it written: "All His paths are pleasant, and all His ways are peaceful?" Is it right for you to hurt your own family? To bring the police? To make wars? Why does it have to be this way?

CHANA: [*pause.*] What way would you like it to be, Mameh Goldie? What choice have any of you left me?

SHEINHOFF: The children are fine, Chana. They're taken care of. You have my word. What is it you want?

CHANA: All I've ever wanted: to do the right thing. Please believe me, Mameh Goldie.

Outside MALE VOICES *threaten:* "*Pritza* (whore), *Sotah* (pervert)!"

SHEINHOFF: You hear? The right thing, Chana, is for you to leave here now, quietly. What was, was. The rift is too deep to heal, and the clock can't be turned back. If you insist on continuing, who knows where you will drag us all…. Go Chana. That's the best thing for you and for the children.

45

CHANA *stares at* SHEINHOFF: *What does she know? What is she afraid of?* SHEINHOFF *does not meet her eyes.*

CHANA: The best thing for my children is to see their mother. You can't imagine....Two years...standing outside the gates of their schools and kindergartens, like a leper, hoping to catch just a glimpse. Running between lawyers and courtrooms, and the money I spent, for a piece of paper....

Music. Children's motif. CHANA *sees them in her imagination, the girls in white. They appear and disappear. They never reach out to her. They are not conscious of her at all.*

CHANA: I should have known Rav Aaron wouldn't honor it, would send his thugs...If it hadn't been for the police, they would have beaten me, too. (SHEINHOFF *mumbles apologetically*) I thought I'd learned to stand up for myself in the last two years. But when my mother and my sister trample over me...I feel like a squashed bug, like that same old doormat...They've even poisoned my daughters against me. It's terrible to see how they're torn....

SHEINHOFF: [*sorrowfully.*] Go, Chanaleh, before the riot starts again.

CHANA: It would be abandoning them again. I just can't. Please!

SHEINHOFF: Nothing you could say would outweigh the harm of doing it this way. Please, if you love them...

CHANA: (*worn down, beginning to give in.*) With all my heart! (Beat) Promise me you'll watch over them, that you won't let my girls be crushed by her, the way she crushed me...And even more, watch over my little ones...

46

SHEINHOFF: You have my word. Show consideration for us now, and who knows? Perhaps in the future something can be worked out.

CHANA: [*after a pause.*] I'll go. For now. But I am not giving up my children. I will never give up my children. I'll think about what to do next and I'll be back. [*she takes her purse, shopping bag, and walks toward the door. Suddenly, with a heartbreaking cry, she turns back and kneels before* SHEINHOFF.] Please, Mameh Goldie!

SHEINHOFF: I can't go against the family.

CHANA: [*heartbroken, she rises, opens her shopping bag. Tearfully.*] This is the doll for Shifraleh, and these are the Chassidic music discs for Shimmy and Shmuel Zanvil, and these are the books for the older boys—[*she drops the bag on the table, unable to speak, turns to leave.*].

SHEINHOFF: [*also in tears. Taking her hand.*] Chana, wait! We can say good-bye like human beings. At least sit a minute. Have a cup of tea before you go [*toward the kitchen.*] Bluma!

BLUMA *enters.*

SHEINHOFF: Bring a cup of tea for your mother.

BLUMA *exits.* FRUME *peeks into the room questioningly.*

[SHEINHOFF *waving her away. In an angry whisper:*] She's going in a minute! [FRUME *disappears.* SHEINHOFF *gropes for a chair.*] Sometimes, that woman makes my head spin…. [*sits.*]

BLUMA *returns with two cups of tea. She serves* SHEINHOFF, *and gives her a questioning look concerning* CHANA'S *cup.*

47

SHEINHOFF: [*indicating a place at opposite end of table.*] Sit in your place, Chana.

CHANA *sits. Pause.* BLUMA *places the cup in front of her.*

BLUMA: [*standing.*] With a teaspoon and a half of sugar.

CHANA: Just as I like it. You remembered. [*taking a sip.*] It looks good on you, the head covering, Bluma. [*taking out her gift.*] I brought you a silk one. It's your favorite color—sky blue. [BLUMA *doesn't take it.*] Come, sit.

BLUMA *looks at* SHEINHOFF, *who nods her approval. She sits near her mother, leaving some distance between them.*

CHANA: [*hurt.*] How is your husband? [*no answer.*] Are you... happy?

BLUMA: [*hedging.*] I accept God's will. One shouldn't complain.

CHANA: In which yeshiva is he learning?

BLUMA: [*angry.*] He isn't learning. He has a job in a printing plant. He learns in the evenings.

CHANA: [*placatingly.*] So you'll have an income. Not every man has to be a scholar. You'll have time to raise your children, when they come, God willing.

BLUMA *raises her head, startled, embarrassed, then looks away.*

CHANA: Blumeleh really? Oh, may God grant you an easy birth at a favorable hour. [*goes to embrace her.*]

BLUMA: [*repulsing her.*] Ssh! Rav Aaron says we shouldn't speak of it for the first three months because of the Evil Eye.

CHANA: Do you believe everything Rav Aaron tells you?

BLUMA: Who can I believe? You won't even be here when I need you.

CHANA: [*sighs.*] I've failed you. When you were born, my eldest, I had such plans; I wanted to be the perfect mother ....

BLUMA: Yes. [*with irony.*] You were always so busy being so perfect behind the piles of ironing, the mountains of dishes. You never had time for us. It was a factory...!

SHEINHOFF: [*cutting her off.*] This is no way to speak to your mother! Besides, this is the way of our world. I'm surprised at you, Bluma! ... [*calling*] Shaineleh! Come, take away the cups. [SHAINE RUTH *enters.*] Go say good-bye to your mother. She's leaving.

BLUMA: [*to* CHANA, *in a whisper.*] I don't want anyone to know!

SHAINE RUTH: [*helplessly.*] Good-bye, *Ima.*

CHANA: [*with mixed emotions.*] Sit with us a moment. [*to* SHEIN-HOFF.] Is that all right? [SHEINHOFF *nods her consent.* CHANA *sits her daughters down on either side of her by the table.* SHAINE RUTH *does so with enthusiasm.* BLUMA *with reservations. All of them are conscious of the ghosts of past family gatherings around this table. Pause. To* SHAINE RUTH.] Tell me, how you are managing with the children?

SHAINE RUTH: Both grandmothers help me. And Bluma.

CHANA: Do they talk about me, sometimes?

BLUMA: They are not big talkers.

49

SHAINE RUTH: [*joyously.*] Moishele acts like a yeshiva boy, and Yitzchak's gotten three inches taller—

CHANA: My brilliant little Talmud scholars! And my red-headed twins, Ruchele and Faigele? For their beautiful long hair. [*takes out pretty hair clips.*]

SHAINE RUTH: [*slightly embarrassed.*] We had to cut it short. There was no time to braid it every morning.

CHANA: Oh, their lovely hair!

BLUMA: Their hair will grow. They are perfectly fine.

SHAINE RUTH: [*breaking in.*] Except—Eliahu has asthma.

CHANA: [*worried.*] What? From when?

BLUMA: [*angry.*] From when you left. But with his medicine, he's fine.

CHANA: [*sadly.*] My children…. Do they wonder…ask…about me?

BLUMA *and* SHAINE RUTH *exchange guilty glances.*

SHAINE RUTH: Not like they used to….

BLUMA: Sometimes.

SHEINHOFF: Chana, it's time.

CHANA: I hope that you bought Moishele and Shmuel Zanvil the bikes for their birthday. That was what they wanted before I—

BLUMA: Out of the charity Rav Aaron collects for *Aba*, it's impossible to buy such luxuries.

CHANA: [*flabbergasted.*] But what about the money I sent them for their birthdays, for all your birthdays, and the money for Chanukah presents every year. Didn't you get it? [SHAINE RUTH: *indicates no.* SHEINHOFF *looks away.*] And my letters—you read the little ones my letters, didn't you? Bluma? Shaine Ruth? [*no response. Understanding dawns.*] He didn't give them to you....

BLUMA: Father knows what's right.

CHANA: I'm not surprised they don't ask about me...

SHEINHOFF: Chana, you have no idea what went on here. It was the price we had to pay to help the children heal. Please, go now. Quietly.

> CHANA *goes toward the door. She picks up a pacifier. Music. Children's motif. They pass by and vanish.*

CHANA: [*to herself, absorbing the full impact.*] Two years. Not a single letter....not one birthday present....nothing. [*to* SHEINHOFF, *accusingly.*] To make them think *I'd* forgotten them.

> *Behind* CHANA'S *back, the* WOMEN *enter quietly from the kitchen.*

CHANA: You lied to me, Mameh Goldie. My children are not fine. They're suffering. [*urgently, pleading.*] You must let me see them. Just for a few minutes. What harm could I do to them in just a few minutes? I will just tell them that I never stopped thinking about them and loving them, and then I'll go. No one has to know! Please, I'm begging you, in the name of that love we've always felt for each other. I can't leave this way...!

GITTE LEAH: So *we'll* leave.

CHANA *panic stricken, turns around and sees the* WOMEN *behind her.*

FRUME: You're right, daughter. Come girls.

ETA: Come Tovah, the time is short and the work is tall...long... great—

CHANA: [*shouting.*] No! No one is going anywhere until I see my children!

GITTE LEAH: Come, come. It's time to go, girls. Let her sit here and wait for her police to come rescue her. Unlike her, I have a family waiting for me.

SHEINHOFF: [*getting up.*] Adinaleh, we'll also go. There's nothing more we can do to help her...

The WOMEN *stand ready to leave. The musical motif of the children fades out.*

CHANA: [*desperately.*] Wait! Wait a minute. I have an idea. Maybe... maybe we can make some kind of deal.

GITTE LEAH: A deal? What is this, the marketplace?

ETA: [*to* TOVAH.] *Vus is dus* (what is this)? What does she want?

TOVAH: To make a sale.... [*shrugs.*]

SHEINHOFF: Quiet! Why is it impossible to listen and speak like human beings? Chanaleh, what are you suggesting?

CHANA: [*thinking fast.*] "Deal" is not the right word. I can't think of the right word just now.... But all of you want me to leave here quietly, true? I understand that, and I'll go, I promise, only listen to me first. That's all I ask.

GITTE LEAH: That's your deal? It's no wonder your clothing business went bankrupt.

FRUME: She thinks that we're merchandise that she can buy or sell.

Pause.

SHEINHOFF: [*concerned.*] That's what you want Chana, to talk?

CHANA: Yes, and for all of you to listen, honestly. It's not much. All I ever wanted in life was to be a mother. You've stolen the dearest wish of my soul. Don't I at least deserve the right to change your minds? Aren't you at least curious to know the truth?

GITTE LEAH: Yankele told the truth to the Rabbinical Court.

CHANA: Did you hear what he said?

GITTE LEAH: A God-fearing woman doesn't get mixed up men's business.

FRUME: My wise daughter. [*to* CHANA.] And the Rabbis judged you and found you guilty and gave you your divorce.

The WOMEN *continue toward the door.*

CHANA: The Rabbis never let me open my mouth. They gave me my divorce and closed the case. The men looked after their own interests. They didn't give me justice! You—you women—can do it. Here. Now. [*impulsively.*] Why don't *you* judge me? You put me on trial!

FRUME *is silent.* CHANA *has touched a nerve. Pause.*

TOVAH: Is it permissible for us to sit in judgment?

ETA: Is it permissible for women?

ADINA: Many things are permitted to women that we don't allow ourselves.... It's permissible for women to learn, and to judge. Deborah the Prophetess was the judge of all Israel.

ETA: She knows. She is learned.

TOVAH: [*dismissively.*] When you have no husband and children to take care of, what else does a woman have to do with herself?

ADINA: [*hurt. Pointedly.*] It's permissible for women to use their brains, Tovah, that is—if they have any. It's not a sin. [*to all.*] Yes, it's permissible for us to hear Chana and judge her. [*looking around.*] It's too bad we don't have a *minyan*. It would give our judgment even greater force.

ETA: A *minyan* means ten men! Who ever heard of a *minyan* of women?!

ADINA: It's permissible for women to hold a *minyan* for secular matters!

FRUME: [*to all.*] What is all this silliness? [*to* CHANA.] We already have the decision of the Rabbinical Court against you.

CHANA: And *another* that reverses it! You respect the first, but tear up the second as worthless! [*taking the plunge.*] Well, I'm ready to give up both Rabbinical decisions, on condition that you yourselves judge me!

Pause.

GITTE LEAH: Don't start with her. She'll lie for hours. I know her. All Meah Shearim will be under our window, witnessing our shame. All I need is for my husband to find out. The ADMOR's wife in such a situation!

Music, the SACRED OATH MOTIF. CHANA *takes a Bible and stands behind the table. A halo of light surrounds her. The change from reality to ritual has begun.*

CHANA: [*with self-control.*] I, Chana Kashman, take a sacred oath in the name of God who is in Heaven to speak only the truth, all of it. And further.... [*with great effort.*] I, Chana Kashman, take an oath. in the name of God who is in Heaven to accept upon myself your verdict. [*she kisses the Bible, and places it on the table.*]

General surprise. Confusion. Pause. SACRED OATH MOTIF *rises.*

ADINA: She took a sacred oath. We are required to listen to her. There are things that only she—that only the woman—knows. In the Book of Samuel, Eli the Priest saw a woman in the Holy Temple acting strangely. He thought she was drunk and cursed her. But when she was allowed to explain, he understood she was simply drunk with grief at being childless. And in the end, he blessed her.

GITTE LEAH: Because she had a good reason for her behavior. What possible reason can Chana have?

ADINA: If we listen, maybe we'll know....

SHEINHOFF: [*evasively.*] Really, Adina. What is there to know? What is there to tell? Everything is clear. [*to* CHANA.] Chanaleh, you know our Torah forbids us to take oaths....

CHANA: But under special circumstances, it's a *mitzvah*. It's an expression of our faith in the justice of God. If you believe in His justice, as I do, you must also swear as I have. Bind yourself with a sacred oath before God to listen with honesty and decide with righteousness!

SHEINHOFF: We are all God-fearing women, who love our Creator and seek to follow His just, compassionate, and merciful ways. It's forbidden for us to take God's name in vain, to swear a sacred oath for some kind of game....

CHANA: It's not a game! It's my life! If I am risking everything by binding myself with an oath, you have to do the same.

GITTE LEAH: [*skeptically.*] What are *you* risking?

CHANA: I told you: If you judge me honestly and righteously and decide I'm unworthy of ever seeing my children again, I.... [*pause, conscious of the terrible risk.*] I will accept your verdict.

Pause. SACRED OATH MOTIF *becomes insistent.* ADINA *approaches the table, picks up the Bible.*

ADINA: I, Adina Sheinhoff, Chana's sister-in-law, accept upon myself a sacred oath to listen to Chana honestly, and to judge her righteously. [*kisses Bible and returns it to table.*]

SHAINE RUTH: [*running to pick up the Bible.*] I, Shaine Ruth, Chana's daughter, accept upon myself a sacred oath to listen to my mother honestly, and to judge her righteously.

BLUMA: I, Bluma, also agree to take upon myself a sacred oath and

swear to listen to mother honestly and to judge her righteously.

ETA: It's not a sin?

ADINA: Only if you don't mean it.

ETA: [*with a cautious glance at Frume, taking the Bible.*] I, Eta Leibowitz, an excellent cook, accept upon myself a sacred oath to
listen to Chana honestly and to decide righteously. Tovah?

TOVAH: I also take this sacred oath upon myself to listen to Chana
honestly and to decide righteously. [*belatedly.*] Tovah Klein,
head attendant at the ritual baths in Geulah.

SACRED OATH MOTIF *reaches crescendo. Cut.*

CHANA: [*taking the Bible to* FRUME.] Madame Kashman.

FRUME: Do you really trust her to leave here quietly when she loses?

ADINA: Mrs. Kashman, the punishment for breaking her oath would be terrible!

GITTE LEAH: You think that would stand in her way? Why, when she was little, Mother had no choice but to punish her a thousand times but still she...

FRUME: [*cutting her off.*] Please. Dirty laundry you wash behind closed doors; not in the middle of the living room.

GITTE LEAH: [*loudly.*] I can't believe how you've all just given in to her! Such a mistake!

ADINA: [*to* GITTE.] Shouting the loudest doesn't make you the smartest.

GITTE LEAH: [*cruelly.*] Maybe I shout. But at least I don't stu...stt...ter!

CHANA: Don't let it bother you, Adina. If Gitte Leah doesn't like you, it's a good sign of your character. [*to* FRUME.] Madame Kashman!

FRUME: Stop already with the "Madame Kashman!" I'm your mother! Your *MOTHER!!!*

CHANA: You were never my mother. You were Gitte Leah's mother. For me, you were always: Madame Kashman, my warden.

GITTE LEAH: Don't you dare speak this way to our mother, you ingrate!

FRUME: All your childhood, all you ever did was cause me pain. Only I know the real Chana Kashman.

CHANA: [*pushing the Bible toward her insistently.*] Swear!

FRUME: [*repulsing her.*] All right, all right. Talk if you want. I don't need Bibles and sacred oaths.

GITTE LEAH: [*surprised and appalled.*] Mother?

FRUME: Yes, why not? What do I have to hide? She wants to try out her lies, we'll listen then go our way. [*to* CHANA.] You have my word of honor.

CHANA: You must swear like all the others. Repeat after me: "I, Frume Kashman, accept upon myself a sacred oath to listen honestly to every word my daughter Chana says and to judge with righteousness whether she should be permitted to see her children again."

SACRED OATH MOTIF *begins again, quietly.*

FRUME: [*repeating the oath.*] I, Frume Kashman accept upon myself a sacred oath to listen honestly to every word Chana says and to judge with righteousness and true justice if she should be forbidden....

CHANA: [*correcting her.*] permitted.

FRUME: [*bristling with rage.*] *Permitted* to see her children again. Oh, what foolishness.... Are you happy now?

CHANA: All of you are my witnesses! [*turns to* GITTE LEAH *with Bible.*]

GITTE LEAH: I don't have to play this game.

CHANA: For once in your life, why don't you try to act like a sister?

59

GITTE LEAH: How dare you! Who took you in when you ran away from home? I was newly married, and instead of preparing myself for life as a great scholar's wife, I had you on my hands to deal with.

CHANA: All right. In that case, you can prepare yourself for life in jail. [*goes to the phone.*]

GITTE LEAH: [*scoffingly.*] *You're* going to put *me* into jail?

CHANA: Yes, Gitte Leah. Outside of Meah Shearim, everyone is equal under the law. And even a great scholar's wife can go to jail if she's convicted of kidnapping. And when you are rotting in prison, the *police* will bring me the children that *I* gave birth to and *I* raised!

General panic.

ETA and TOVAH: [*stuttering, appalled. Jail?*] Sorry. We just came to borrow some vinegar. Oil. For the compote. Potato kugel.

SHEINHOFF: This is what you want, Chana? That they be brought to you by force, in a police car? Do you want to shame *and* frighten them to death?

CHANA: It's not what I want. But what other choice is she leaving me? [*she dials.*] "Police?"

GITTE LEAH: Stop it! (*Takes the phone and slams it down.*) Stop it already. All right. (*She takes the Bible*) For the good of the family, not like you, to get rid of the Cossacks, I, Gitte Leah, take a sacred oath to listen honestly to Chana and to decide righteously. (*Kisses the Bible and lays it down.*) And after the humiliations you've put us through—your own sister. your own mother!—don't dream of crawling back to us for help when you finally land where you deserve—in the gutter.

CHANA: Shut up! I'm not your house slave anymore, Gitte Leah. You've sworn to listen, so listen! Now, it's my turn to speak.

FRUME: Nu! So talk already, so we can get this over and done with.

GITTE LEAH: Today, if it's not too much to ask. The rest of us have lives to get back to.

SHAINE RUTH: [*quietly, to* SHEINHOFF.] *Mameh* Goldie, did you take your oath?

BLUMA: Of course she did!

CHANA: [*to* SHEINHOFF.] Shaine Ruth is right. We forgot about you [*holds out the Bible*].

SHEINHOFF: [*takes Bible reluctantly, shaking her head.*] Chanaleh, why don't you listen to me? Let the wounds heal, I tell you, instead of scraping away at them, causing more pain. If you insist on doing this your way, who knows where it will end...

As SHEINHOFF *speaks, the* SHOUTS *outside increase. The women's attention is diverted.* SHAINE RUTH *goes to the window.*

SHAINE RUTH: Look at that woman! She's gone *meshugah*. To fight her way through all those men. They'll kill her!

WOMEN *and* CHANA *hurry to the window. Now their backs are to* SHEINHOFF, *who stares indecisively at the Bible, then puts it down without taking the oath. Outside, the tumult increases, shouts of* "Pritzah! Zonah! *and* Sotah!" *are heard.*

SHAINE RUTH: [*at window.*] It's Zehava! She's gotten through! She's coming upstairs!

CHANA *is the first to run to the front door.* WOMEN *mill around helplessly. In the melee, no one notices* SHEINHOFF *has not sworn her oath.*

Scene five

CHANA *opens the door. Enter* ZEHAVA, *disheveled and injured. The* WOMEN *cringe from her, distancing themselves.*

CHANA: *Rebono shel olam* (Lord of the Universe)! Zehava! [*taking care of her.*] Criminals!

ZEHAVA: What about you? All Meah Shearim is talking about what they are going to do to you. I couldn't sit home. I just couldn't.

CHANA: [*bitterly.*] I'm all right.

ZEHAVA: Why didn't you call? I didn't know what to think when you took so long. It's hard for you to say good-bye to the children...

CHANA: Zehava...[*on the verge of tears.*] They've hidden them.

ZEHAVA *hugs* CHANA. *The* WOMEN *are scandalized, misinter-*

preting this supportive gesture as something sexual. FRUME *covers* SHAINE RUTH'S *eyes.*

FRUME: [*to* CHANA *and* ZEHAVA.] May God strike you both dead, you shameless creatures!

CHANA: Remember her, Zehava? Madame Kashman.

ZEHAVA: Of course, your mother. Shalom [*extends her hand.*].

FRUME: [*spits and turns away.*] You came here to flaunt your perversions...

CHANA: [*cutting her off.*] What?! Perversions!? Girls! Go bring some antiseptic and bandages.

Exit BLUMA *and* SHAINE RUTH. CHANA *seats* ZEHAVA *and treats her wounds.*

GITTE LEAH: Don't play the saint with us. A woman who loves another woman. We're not so innocent here, we know what you are—Latvians! (*mispronunciation of "lesbians".*)

ZEHAVA: [*defiant.*] Yes, I love Chana. She is my sister, my mother, my friend. As long as I live, I will never desert her the way you have.

GITTE LEAH *insulted, exits.*

ZEHAVA: [*mockingly.*] Who started these rumors? Eta? Tovah?

ETA and TOVAH: [*reluctantly.*] Hello Zehava, how are you?

FRUME: [*looking daggers at* ETA *and* TOVAH.] You are also friends of this degenerate?

ETA: God Forbid!

TOVAH: We're practically strangers.

ETA: [*to* FRUME.] She used to join us when Chana gave us classes on a woman's role in the family.

TOVAH: We don't know anything about her.

ETA: Only that she has ten children, and one of them is autistic, and her parents forced her to marry a man twenty years older who beat her and she's had dozens of miscarriages and was just about ready to kill herself when....

TOVAH: Shhh! [*elbows her.*] Chana brought her.

ETA: It was Chana's doing. She knows her.

> BLUMA *and* SHAINE RUTH *enter with first-aid.* CHANA *takes care of* ZEHAVA'S *wounds.*

ZEHAVA: [*with derision to* TOVAH *and* ETA.] Such dishrags!

CHANA: [*as she dabs Zehava's wounds.*] They can't even imagine a real friendship between women; that one woman would stand by another even when she's being shunned, would take her in when she's homeless, would take the blows meant for her on her own body....

ETA: [*to* TOVAH, *in a whisper.*] The Modesty Patrol, two years ago, did you forget? They broke into the house, beat her, *farshteyst?* Broke her hand—

TOVAH:—and her leg!

FRUME: Her head they should have broken...

ZEHAVA: Believe me they tried, Mrs. Kashman. They came to take Chana back to her husband by force, but "the poor things," they only found me. One beat me with a bat but still I wouldn't tell them anything. The second one would have killed me if I hadn't sat down on him until the police came. Thank God for blessing me with a healthy appetite and something to show for it. I'd do anything for her....

ETA: Of course you would, because you and she [*waggling two fingers at her, to indicate their sexual relations.*]

TOVAH: Exactly.

CHANA: [*while taking care of* ZEHAVA.] Didn't I say it? They don't trust friendship, just wicked gossip. A whisper here, a raised eyebrow there...It's enough to explode an entire life of good deeds. They do it in the synagogue during the Torah reading, or waiting for their turn to purify themselves in the ritual baths....

TOVAH: [*with righteous denial.*] Gossip, in my ritual baths...?

CHANA: [*cynically.*] I know, I know. You don't permit gossip.

ETA: [*defensively.*] Someone from the yeshiva said Rav Aaron himself saw you dressed like a slut walking down Ben Yehuda street...

CHANA: So, our saintly Rabbi, our uncle, was standing out on street corners staring at women?

FRUME: [*to* BLUMA *and* SHAINE RUTH.] Girls! Stop up your ears!

CHANA: No one ever saw me dressed immodestly. When I was fifteen years old, I gave myself permission to be anything I wanted, and I *chose* to be a religious woman because I loved God.

66

[*pointing to window.*] And no wheeler-dealer who calls himself a Rabbi can change that!

ZEHAVA: It doesn't surprise me that the men are behind all these rumors. [*getting up to leave.*] They're terrified we women will band together and give each other strength. So, to keep us weak, they make us suspicious of one another. They enforce marriage and divorce laws that keep us chained like prisoners to men we despise. A man doesn't need a gun to kill a wife. He can squeeze the life out of her drop by drop.... [*heavy silence.*] Come, let's go Chana. From them [*contemptuously.*] you'll get nothing. [*her wounds are dressed. She turns to leave.*]

CHANA: I can't. Not yet.

ZEHAVA: Why? Your children aren't even here.

Enter GITTE LEAH.

CHANA: They've sworn to listen. Once they hear the truth, they'll have to let me see them.

ZEHAVA: Don't—Chana! Don't give them another chance to step all over you! You've got a court order!

ADINA: Wait! [*counts.*] Now we have a *minyan.*

SHAINE RUTH: [*counting.*] Right! With Zehava we're ten.

ETA: *Naye rabonim hobn nisht keyn minyen. Tsen shotn hobn a minyen.*

[*To* ZEHAVA:] *Farshteyst?* Understand?

ZEHAVA: No.

ETA: A Jew who doesn't know Yiddish? A *shiksa!*

ZEHAVA: [*ironically*] No. Just a Moroccan…

ADINA: It means nine rabbis are not a minyan—

ETA:—but ten fools are!

SHAINE RUTH: [*brings* CHANA *the Bible.*] *Ima,* she has to swear.

ADINA: All of us have already taken a sacred oath.

SHEINHOFF *shrinks in her place.*

CHANA: Zehava, it's my only chance of seeing the children today. Please, swear! [*holds out the Bible.*]

ZEHAVA: This is a terrible mistake, Chana [*she sighs.*]. All right, all right, God help us….

CHANA: I, Zehava Toledano, accept upon myself this sacred oath—

ZEHAVA: I, Zehava Toledano, accept upon myself this sacred oath—

CHANA:—to listen to Chana honestly and to judge her righteously.

ZEHAVA: With all my heart, to listen to my friend Chana with honesty and to judge her righteously.

Music. MOTIF OF THE OATH. CHANA *begins to pray. The change from reality to ritual.*

INTERMISSION.

Act II

Prologue

The women stand behind the table. Before each is a basin and a two-handed ritual cup. In unison, they grasp the cup in their left hand, and pour water twice over their right fist, repeating with the other hand. A beam of light touches each one. They fade. A halo of light surrounds the table, widens and encircles the stage. The realistic room disappears. The women move outside the circle. CHANA *stands alone in the center, her eyes closed, she prays. The* MAN'S VOICE *who has read the laws in the opening scene, returns to do battle with the power of the women's minyan, delegitimizing it to weaken and demean them.* CHANA's *prayer does battle with it, overcoming and silencing it, fending off the male intrusion into the women's mystical circle, the sacred oath that now binds them.*

MALE VOICE: A group of ten men of Israel, over the age of thirteen, are a "congregation", a society, a *minyan* for the purposes of public prayer or other holy activities. Even if one hundred women pray together, they have no authority to perform a sacred act. They may not publicly declare God's Oneness. They may not lead the congregation in prayer. They may not

71

perform the Priestly blessing, or a public reading of the Torah or of the Prophets. They may not convene a public event or a council. They may not publicly comfort the mourner or bless the bridegroom or say grace after meals because, as it is written: "I will be blessed amongst the Children of Israel," and throughout the entire Torah, the "Children of Israel" refers to free, male adults. A woman is a *golem*, a lump of clay, without stature, who cannot make a covenant with God, and therefore, cannot join a *minyan*.

CHANA: [*fighting back, with prayer.*] To You, O Lord, do I lift up my soul. In You, O God, have I put my trust; do not let me be deceived. Do not let my enemies triumph. Let me find my way in Your truth. Teach me, for You are the God of my salvation, and it is for You I wait all day.

MALE VOICE: "Even at a time of affliction for Israel, when individuals abandon the congregation, and doom themselves to hell, even at such a time women may not join a *minyan* to make up ten; even one woman with nine men. A woman does not join a *minyan* even for the purpose of witnessing a public display of martyrdom to sanctify the Holy Name. A woman may not judge, or be a witness. Gentiles, slaves, women, fools, and children are ineligible to give testimony. Women are not called a congregation."

CHANA: [*escalating the battle.*] Behold my enemies, how many they are and how they hate me. Watch over my soul and save me from them, let me not be ashamed that I have trusted in You. Innocence and righteousness will preserve me, for I have put my trust in You.

MALE VOICE: [*beginning to capitulate.*] But ten women can gather together unto themselves for public service, or to read the Scroll of Esther on Purim. Ten women are considered a congregation for lighting candles, for drinking four cups of wine on Passover,

and eating bitter herbs. Ten women are a congregation for the
purpose of reconciling a man to his enemy.

CHANA: [*her prayers partially answered.*] He guides the humble through
judgment, and teaches the humble His way. Thus all the paths
of the Lord are full of truth and loving-kindness to those who
keep His Covenant. For the sake of Your name, Lord, pardon
my iniquity. Troubles have already enlarged my heart—Oh
lead me out of my affliction...For Your mercy is before my
eyes and I have earnestly walked in your truth.

*The circle is formed. The oath binds them all within it until it is
fulfilled. The* WOMEN *who surround* CHANA *turn expectantly
toward her. She is deep in prayer. Her daughters enter the circle,
approaching her.*

SHAINE RUTH: Talk to us, *Ima*! Tell us what happened!

BLUMA: Why did you leave us?

Scene one

CHANA'S *inner monologue, begun as prayer, transforms into confession. To* BLUMA, SHAINE RUTH.

CHANA: [*looking around at the house, as if in a dream.*] Twenty years of my life I gave to this house, hour by hour, day by day. To build something harmonious and good. For twenty years·I held my finger in the dike, to keep the horror around me from flooding through. You never saw, never even suspected. But even a sponge gets full, so full it cannot hold another drop....

    The woman who ran away two years ago was not the mother you knew.... It had nothing to do with you, my innocent children... The dam finally broke.

CHANA *becomes aware of the circle of sacred oath.*

CHANA: I could have cowered—as always—allowed myself to drown. But for some reason, I stood up. A strong urge to live gave me strength I didn't know I had. I turned my back on everything and ran for my life. Only later did the mind wake up, with regrets, pangs of conscience, longings—

FRUME: Who were you running away from?

ADINA: Who was chasing you?

GITTE LEAH: Stories.

TOVAH: You left for her. [*points to* ZEHAVA.]

ETA: Everyone knows.

ZEHAVA: Not one of you knows anything! You swore to listen, so listen!

The WOMEN *grow silent, remembering their sacred oath.*

CHANA: [*focused on her daughters.*] Blumaleh, Shaine Ruth, when I left I never dreamt that it would end this way. The minute I could, I tried to settle everything quickly and quietly so I could come home to you—my children. But you [*pointing to* FRUME.] all of you, blocked my way. The family, the community, my friends [*looking at* ETA *and* TOVAH.] you all stood together against me as I smashed myself again and again against the walls of your hard, cold hearts…

SHEINHOFF: Chana, you gave us no other choice…

FRUME: You left.

GITTE LEAH: It's your own fault.

CHANA: [*bitterly.*] I thought so, too. I tried to figure out where I had gone wrong…what had happened to my marriage and why. It didn't start out bad…. [*looking at her girls.*].

GITTE LEAH: ·Not bad?! Why you ungrateful woman! You didn't deserve a man like Yankele.

FRUME: It was a miracle, such a match: a Talmud scholar, from a most respected family...

GITTE LEAH: His father was an ADMOR...

TOVAH: And his Uncle, Rav Aaron, was on the Council of Torah Sages—

ETA:—and the head of a Yeshiva—*A Grosse Yichoos!* (a great honor).

CHANA: Yes, Yankele was a gift. A match made in heaven.... by accident. I knocked on the wrong door and he opened it. Right after he saw me, he sent matchmakers to talk to my father. You were all so shocked. That such a family would want me! You never dreamed of looking into the background of the distinguished bridegroom. Who was I, after all? The despised failure. My sister was already burning to fix me up with a fat, newly religious Jew, with hairy knuckles and a bald head....

FRUME: She was burning because you'd defiled your honor...

GITTE LEAH: With a soldier! What a disgrace!

ETA: [*scandalized.*] *Vus!?* (what) She was defiled?

TOVAH: By a soldier!!!?

GITTE LEAH: A soldier she met with all her running around. [*to* CHANA] You swore to tell the truth, so tell it!

> GITTE LEAH *enters the circle and swivels* CHANA *around like a boxer in the ring.*

CHANA: [*with sarcasm.*] A soldier? Why not the whole platoon? The entire army? [*to everyone, bitterly.*] The truth was, a miracle happened. I was defiled by a letter.

Shocked, aggressive responses.

GITTE LEAH: [*to everyone, disgusted.*] Aren't you ashamed to speak like that?! [*to all.*] Under my roof, she got a letter from a soldier. An envelope from the army came to the house of the ADMOR!

CHANA: [*dripping with sarcasm.*] God save us! With an official army stamp which proved—beyond a reasonable doubt—that Chana had committed a mortal sin. Who cared that inside the envelope was a scientific paper? Or that it was from a soldier who started to speak to me on a train to Haifa because he'd never in his life spoken to a religious girl before? When I told him I was interested in science too, that I was reading books underneath my blanket at night because the ADMOR—your husband—didn't approve of secular studies for girls.

GITTE LEAH: Profanity, that's what you brought into the house of the saintly ADMOR. Filth.

CHANA: [*patiently.*]—the soldier told me he was working on a project to turn salt water into drinking water, and offered to send me his paper on the subject…

GITTE LEAH: When a woman opens her mind, a lot of garbage gets thrown in.…

CHANA: You can't really believe that, Gitte Leah. You're just jealous that I had the courage to use the brain that the Holy One, Blessed be He, gave me.

GITTE LEAH: Did you want my husband—the ADMOR—to find the letter? Was that it? You knew how he made my life hell with all his stringencies. Did you want to ruin my marriage completely?

CHANA: All you had to do was ask me. Instead, you started screaming

78

and ran off with the envelope to Madame.... [*to everyone.*] who immediately called a meeting of the family council of geniuses and holy men.... And they decided that there was nothing left to do but marry the sinner off—and fast. So, after I refused my sister's hairy fat candidate, Madame dredged up a hairless skinny one, with pale clammy skin and a wispy beard, that knew all about the world from what he read in the Kosher Food Bulletin, if he read at all...

FRUME: [*entering the circle, turning alternately to* CHANA *and the* WOMEN.] Ah, so the sought-after prize of Meah Shearim said no. The matchmakers' dream girl refused. The whole family was wrong, the whole ultra-Orthodox world was wrong, only she was right. Just like now. Leaving her husband and children is only her latest sin....

GITTE LEAH: Don't overstrain yourself, Mother.

FRUME: You don't know what it was like to raise such a rebellious child! [*to* CHANA] Tell them, everything, from the beginning, the whole truth: How you were wild and full of *chutzpah*; how you did everything that came into your head. Tell them how you lied right and left, tell them how you stole!

ETA and TOVAH: [*shocked.*] A thief? A *ganeveta?* (thief) *May God watch over us!*

CHANA: [*sadly ironic.*] Yes, I admit it. I stole. [*beat.*] A handful of raisins from a jar that Madame kept on a shelf above *my* bed, specially for Gitte Leah, her favorite.

GITTE LEAH: It wasn't only my raisins—

CHANA: Still the same sniveling, sanctimonious tattletale...! Yes, I admit it. I also stole money from Madame's purse. Some pennies to buy lollipops. I was four and already corrupt...

[Reactions: Thou shall not steal]

—and Madame caught me and did what she knew how to do best: take out my father's belt and deliver a few lashes on my behind, and a few on my back, and a few on my small legs that were trying to run away. She beat and beat and beat, until the "thief" fainted.

CHANA *collapses.* ZEHAVA *hurries to help her.*

SHAINE RUTH: *Ima, Ima* [BLUMA *checks her.*]

FRUME: "He who spares the rod, hates his child." My own mother threw me into an orphanage when she was widowed, but I put my whole life into this child. To change her from a weak-willed thief into a strong, honest, decent.... But in the end it was no use. Just like my own mother, she also threw away her children because she thought only of herself.... [*to* CHANA.] A child is not a suitcase that you leave behind and come back for when you feel like it.

SHEINHOFF: May Hashem watch over us. Frume!

FRUME: [*furious.*] Everything she was taught she had to question. "Why can't I go to a school that prepares for matriculation exams?" Imagine, going to college, a religious girl! "Why do men thank God for not making them a woman?" Always, she had to be smarter than everybody else. So smart she was she couldn't find her way to the bathroom at night. [*to* CHANA.] You swore to tell the truth, so tell them how you wet the bed until you were practically Bat Mitzvah....

CHANA: [*supported by* ZEHAVA.] Was it any wonder after all those beatings? Lying in bed, afraid more would come. And they came, the beatings...even though I washed your floors, and

polished your silver, and peeled your potatoes to win your love—all I ever got was the belt.

ADINA: What cruelty!

CHANA: No, Adina. Cruelty is when you take a child's hand [*takes* FRUME's *hand*] and lead her out into the street in her soaked nightgown, stopping neighbors to complain how stupid she is, and how wonderful her older sister is. [*she looks down at her hand.*] While the child stands there, trying to convince herself she's a piece of wood, without ears or eyes or a heart....

FRUME, *embarrassed, confused, throws off* CHANA's *hand.* BLUMA, SHAINE RUTH *stare at* FRUME, *appalled.*

FRUME: Shame makes us fear sin. I did to you what my mother did to me, and her mother did to her. My husband refused to punish his pretty daughter, so I was forced to teach her some self-discipline. Your father just spoiled you. He was weak.

CHANA: You were always jealous of the love he gave me. Behind your back, he sent me signals...encouragement. I only survived because of him.

The circle moves in the opposite direction. BLUMA *suddenly enters the circle facing* CHANA.

BLUMA: What does any of this have to do with *us*? With what you did to *us*?

SHAINE RUTH: Bluma, don't!

BLUMA: [*hugging her sister, but undeterred.*] You tell us that Granny Frume was a terrible mother? She didn't give you things? She hit you? Well, you were much worse. You ran away! Who do you think had to take care of your children while you went looking for happiness? We did, the "older" girls…Older…

SHAINE RUTH *tries once again to make her stop, and is repulsed.*

BLUMA: I was seventeen years old. I still needed a mother. Instead, I had to become one for ten children. You always taught us we had to make choices in life. But you didn't give us any. You were a grown, educated woman…. You had a choice, yet you chose to abandon us, to blacken our name. You chose to ruin my chances to marry the man I wanted, a scholar, Joseph Graetz. And now you've come back to ruin Shaine Ruth's chances. [*to* SHAINE RUTH.] Tell her! Say something! [*to* CHANA.] This was *your* choice, *Ima*. So, now I get to choose. And I choose not to know you. You are nothing to me anymore. A stranger.

CHANA: [*in pain.*] It wasn't a choice, Blumaleh. It was a matter of life or death. But how could you have known…? I did everything to hide what was happening between me and your father….

BLUMA: Don't you dare blame Father! You ran and he stayed. For Father, the Torah is his whole life, yet he took care of us instead of you. Father is a model of righteousness! [*returns to the outer circle.*]

Outside, MEN'S VOICES *are heard praying. Their presence seeps inside the room full of women, a constant, dominating force that surrounds them.*

Scene two

The circle turns and stops. Memory comes and retreats. CHANA *is alone.*

CHANA: The model of righteousness. Yes…When I met him, he was [*beat.*]…Yankele Sheinhoff, the brilliant Talmud scholar. The first time we went out alone, he said he wanted to touch me. I knew it was forbidden to say such things. But I thought: How wonderful. He's studied so much. He knows the truth outside the rules. He'll teach me. We'll spend our lives together, learning and growing. Together we'll discover the secrets of life. We married—in happiness. I was happy, even though I didn't know what to expect. I'd never once touched a man. On our wedding night, I sat in our hotel room waiting. Finally, Yankele came over and asked me: What are you waiting for? And I answered: I read in a holy book that it is better for the bride to feel desire before she does the mitzva. And so I'm sitting here, waiting to feel some.…

Reactions of sympathy, laughter.

CHANA: He also laughed.

SHEINHOFF: You were such a beautiful couple.

ETA: It was a match made in heaven.

TOVAH: You looked so happy together.

CHANA: Yes. We kept up appearances.... And maybe, in the beginning, I was content. From a humiliated child I became the honored Rabbi's wife: *Rebbitzen* Chana Sheinhoff. All the rabbis sent me women to advise. Yankele learned Torah, and I built the family. I took care of supporting us by working at odd jobs, and tried to keep up my studies in the evenings. But most of all, I gave birth.... [*looks with pride at her daughters*].

TOVAH: [*enters the circle. To* CHANA.] I remember how you came to the ritual bath for the first time. Like all the young brides, just a little older than children they are, their skin so pink and creamy, their bodies supple and beautiful. And then, God be blessed, they get pregnant. Years go by, you wouldn't recognize them. Their eyes are dull, their bodies bloated and neglected and tired. All those beautiful young brides....

SHEINHOFF: This is God's will, the purpose of woman's creation....

CHANA: [*to daughters.*] I never regretted a single one of you. You filled my life with joy. Willingly, I gave you my soul. I was prepared to work endlessly. Twelve children!! Soon enough I understood that I had no choice; that I was in this all alone. Yankele made a separate life for himself. He spent his time in the yeshiva, or else alone in his study. He would disappear suddenly, I had no idea where.... I started to feel as if I was rolling a great rock up a mountain alone and with every step it threatened to roll back and crush me....

FRUME: All of us work hard for our homes and our children. It's God's will.

ZEHAVA: No, Mrs. Kashman, it's the men's will. In our marriage contracts it's written that the husband has to support his wife. That's Jewish law.

Shocked reactions. It is the societal norm for women to support their husbands so that they may study.

GITTE LEAH: [*haughty and indignant.*] The letter of the law. *By us,* it's a woman's duty and honor to be the helpmate of a Torah scholar, if you don't mind.

TOVAH: [*superior. To* ZEHAVA.] Like Joseph's brothers in the Bible. Zebulun worked so Yissacher could study. "Happy is Zebulun in going out and Yissacher in his tent."

ETA: *She* has to be the breadwinner so that *he* can learn.

GITTE LEAH: And she has to be obedient to the man in everything. You understand?

ADINA: Excuse me, Gitte Leah.... A woman has to be obedient to God and His holy Torah, not to men.

TOVAH: A God-fearing woman accepts the Rabbis interpretation of the Torah, and keeps the commandments as the men explain them. She's like the earth, a receptacle for the holy seed.

ZEHAVA: And like the earth, the men step all over her...

ADINA: Maimonides says that it's man's obligation to love his wife as himself, and to honor her more than himself.

ZEHAVA: True. There has to be love, honor, partnership.

GITTE LEAH: Maimonides doesn't mean what you mean. This whole business of "love" is foolishness for silly girls. A woman with complete faith doesn't look for such things. She's on a higher level.

CHANA: I saw how your ADMOR treats you, there, on that "higher level"…

GITTE LEAH: [*defensively.*] This is our life on this earth! A decent woman doesn't marry for love, but for a family! You serve your husband, give birth to his children, and in exchange you get honor in this world and your portion in the World to Come. Everything else is wantonness for the faithless.

CHANA: If a woman is only a womb, then why did God torture her with intelligence, understanding, creativity, wisdom? Why didn't He make her ant-like, without the consciousness to raise her head and examine her role as a beast of burden?

ZEHAVA: Where is it written that a woman has to give birth every year?

FRUME: "Be fruitful and multiply and replenish the earth." It's the first commandment in the Torah.

ADINA: [*drily.*] I don't think the Torah meant single-handedly. Anyhow, if you'll excuse me Mrs. Kashman, the Torah gives the *mitzvah* of procreation to Adam, not Eve. And it's enough to have two children to fulfill the commandment.

GITTE LEAH: Even that you don't do, so what are you making yourself so wise? "A person with no children is considered dead."

FRUME: Gitte Leah! [*to* SHEINHOFF.] I'm sorry, Goldie. She's in pain so she gets nervous.…

88

GITTE LEAH *mumbles an apology.*

SHEINHOFF: [*in sorrow and admonition.*] With God's help, her turn will come. It's all God's will. Everything is in God's hands.

MALE VOICES *read the Psalms, threateningly.*

Scene three

CHANA, *detached, doesn't take part in the debate. She wavers before jumping into the fray, hesitant to reveal the secrets of her marriage.*

SHAINE RUTH: *Ima*, are you going to continue?

CHANA: [*with effort.*] Yes, yes... I was like Zevulun. I thought: it's my duty to be the model Rabbi's wife. I opened my doors to needy yeshiva boys, arranged lectures for women, guided my friends with pious advice, and never complained, even though I thought I would melt from exhaustion. I obeyed my husband in everything, even when his demands...even when he behaved in a way...a way ...I couldn't understand. His will was done. The important thing was not to fail in my marriage. Except that it wasn't only dependent on me.... I want to stop now.

Reactions. "What is she hinting at?" ZEHAVA *prevents her from withdrawing. They argue.*

ZEHAVA: [*encouragingly.*] Tell about the money. That should be enough.

CHANA: [*nodding assent, she chooses her words carefully.*] When it came time for Bluma to marry, I tried every way I knew to increase our income. Zehava and I decided to open a dress store. My husband, the "model of righteousness", agreed, but on condition that he keep the books and handle the money. The store brought in a good income. Until one day, just like that, our checks began to bounce. The bank stopped payment to our suppliers. Someone had withdrawn all our funds. Sixty thousand shekel. Mine and Zehava's money.

ZEHAVA: I was desperate. I didn't know how I'd feed my children.

SHEINHOFF: What happened? Who could have taken the money?

CHANA: Who had access to the account? [*pause.*] I was shocked.

Mutterings: "Father?" "Yankele?" SHEINHOFF *grows faint.. The* WOMEN *attempt to shield her. But doubt hangs like a sword over their heads. Surprisingly,* SHEINHOFF *rises and enters the circle, confronting* CHANA.

SHEINHOFF: Enough already! [*to* CHANA.] I didn't want to believe what they all said about you, but now I know: Your mother was right. Only she knows the real Chana Kashman. A child who lies and steals, it's in her character, it's forever! And that's what you're doing now, making up disgusting lies about your husband to cover up your own sins. And to think, I always defended you, even here, today! Do you really expect me to believe such a thing about my son?! Never! What a mistake we made in agreeing to listen to you at all.

CHANA: It's the truth, Mameh Goldie. Didn't I take a sacred oath?

FRUME: [*supporting* SHEINHOFF.] A decent woman would have gotten advice from a Rav, but she—!

CHANA: [*fighting for* SHEINHOFF's *support.*] That's *exactly* what I did, Mameh Goldie! Instead of going to the police, I went to a Rav! To the head of my husband's distinguished family—and told him about the theft.

SHEINHOFF: Don't you dare use that word!

CHANA: All right, all right, just listen to me, please! Didn't you all swear you'd hear me out honestly? Unlike you, Rav Aaron believed me. He was very angry at what I told him—and not just about the stealing…"Go home, my daughter," the Rav said. "And don't worry. I'll speak to Yankele and force him to return all he took. And I'll make him treat you according to the laws of our holy Torah. And if he refuses, you have my word, I'll help you get a divorce."

FRUME: [*shocked.*] You spoke of divorce?! On account of some money?

CHANA: That was just the last straw.

FRUME: [*to* CHANA.] Naturally, you didn't give the Rav a chance….

CHANA: I followed his instructions to the letter! I waited in the dress store while the Rav spoke to Yankele. It was late when I finally went home. Shaineleh was setting the table for the holiday. Bluma was ironing the boys' white shirts. I went to Yankele in his study. Looking down at my shoes, humbly, I begged him to at least return a little money to Zehava so she could feed her children. There was silence. I looked at him: there was murder in his eyes. I had ripped away his mask, shown his real face to Rav Aaron!! How dare I!! Before I could answer, he locked the door behind me, threw me on the floor, dragged me to the bed, hit me with his fists, choked me. I thought: this is the end. Now I will die. I don't know how, I managed to get free, to unlock the door....

Shock, confusion. Can they believe? They await the reaction of SHEINHOFF *and* FRUME. BLUMA *and* SHAINE RUTH *lower their gaze—they have seen the evidence with their own eyes.*

SHEINHOFF: [*with great emotion.*] What? What is she saying about my sensitive, gentle son who never raised his hand to hurt a fly...

CHANA: There are many things you don't know about him, Mameh.

SHEINHOFF: But stealing, wife-beating? For years you had a beautiful life together. Overnight he turned into a monster?

CHANA: [*quietly.*] It didn't happen overnight. For years I.... [*stops herself. To* BLUME, SHAINE RUTH.] The children were there. The girls saw how I came out of that room. [*to them.*] I had to escape. My life was in danger. You can tell the truth now!

BLUME, SHAINE RUTH are torn. To implicate their father, admit the disgrace...?

FRUME: Don't forget: I was there too. Didn't I warn you, beg you, not to go? But you wouldn't listen, as usual. You shook us off and ran!

CHANA: [*to daughters.*] Bluma, Shaine Ruth, you heard my screams. You know it's true!

FRUME: Don't answer her, girls! [*to* CHANA.] So maybe he raised his hand to you [*shrugs.*]. These things happen. You made him angry. A family quarrel you settle inside the family! You should have gone back to the Rav instead of running!

ZEHAVA: [*bitterly.*] She did go back. I told her there was no point, but she insisted. She wanted to do everything respectably—for the children. For you, Mrs. Kashman.

Surprised reactions.

CHANA: The Rav saw the bruises. And this time I told him the rest—everything Yankele had done to me over the years. I asked him to help me get a divorce, to keep his word.

ADINA: What was his answer?

ZEHAVA: What they always say to us when they send us home to these men.

CHANA: [*ironically.*] He rubbed his hands together, and smoothed down his beard. "We have ways of dealing with women who slander fine Torah scholars," he warned me. "Stubborn women, women with *chutzpah*. There are doctors who commit them to insane asylums. Modesty Patrols who discipline them. There are two sides to every story. Go home and ask your husband to forgive you, woman."

ADINA: [*incredulous.*] *Him* to forgive *you?!* What did you do?

CHANA: Zehava took me in off the street, endangering her own life. And then, after the holiday, I went to a divorce lawyer. I couldn't go back. I would rather have died. It was the hardest decision of my life.

TOVAH: And every one of us paid the price and continues to pay.

FRUME: In our world there are rules. Women have to obey them. She never understood that!

TOVAH: [*to* CHANA.] It's true. You always tried to convince us that we could change things, but it's impossible.

ETA: As it is written: If the hand hits the rock or the rock hits the hand, *Oy* to the rock .... *farshteyst?*

TOVAH: The opposite! *Oy* to the hand!!

CHANA: It is possible to change things! If we stop hiding, stop pretending. We women are taught to wash away the dirt, and when the messes the men create cannot be bleached, we're taught to take the stains on ourselves so that they can remain spotless. What was my great sin, I ask you? That I couldn't cover up for my husband anymore? That I told the truth? I was the victim, but the community will never forgive me. The sacrificial lamb isn't allowed to climb down off the altar, right? She has to stretch out her neck to the blade.

Pause

Remember the Torah your mothers taught you! Don't let anyone frighten you into calling a sin a mitzvah and a mitzvah a sin. I've kept my oath; I've told the truth. Now you must keep yours. You must decide in justice and righteousness: May I see my children?

The circle continues to turn, as the wome ponder the question.

ADINA: Chana's life was in danger. She had no choice. She was treated unjustly, and now we have the chance to give her justice, all of us. I vote that she be allowed to see her children.

ZEHAVA: [*hurriedly.*] I also vote yes. [*joining* ADINA.]

ADINA: [*to* SHEINHOFF.] *Ima?*

SHEINHOFF *rebuffs her, adamant in her refusal. The others wait for* FRUME'S *reaction.*

FRUME: No. Rav Aaron was right. A woman who destroys her family on account of money? Your children were the victims, not you. Why do you have the right to see them?

ADINA: But he…he stole from her!

GITTE LEAH: That's *her* story.

ADINA: He choked her…threatened to kill her!

SHEINHOFF: [*furious.*] How can you believe this? *You*, his own sister?!

GITTE LEAH: What does it matter what happened between them? A woman has to remain at home. As it is written: "Your wife like

a fruitful vine surrounding your house." In absolutely no case do you break the sacred marriage bonds. The home is above everything. I vote "no."

FRUME: And I. Tovah? Eta?

TOVAH *and* ETA *hesitate. They move toward* FRUME.

Scene four

The scales are weighted against CHANA. ZEHAVA *enters the circle.*

ZEHAVA: NO! Wait! There's no choice. You can't hold back any more. Tell them!

GITTE LEAH: [*to* ZEHAVA.] A degenerate helps a degenerate. The "dress store" was your idea, wasn't it? And it wasn't to make a living, was it? It was so you could come there at night and be with Chana. We all know what for!

FRUME: And now she makes up stories about her husband to cover for you, unnatural woman!

ZEHAVA: [*pleading.*] Tell them. Chana!

CHANA: Please.... How can I speak of such things? [*looking at her daughters.*] My daughters are here, and his mother.... I can't....

ZEHAVA: You have to! Or you'll lose your children!

CHANA: Oh, God in Heaven! You have no idea—[*clutching* ZEHAVA.]

ZEHAVA: Courage, Chana! Tell them everything.

CHANA: The words won't come…. they are stuck in my throat…please, you do it….

ZEHAVA: The store was Chana's refuge. She escaped there to save her body from the pollution of his unnatural acts, the sickening things he forced on her, things he learned from videos he brought home from Tel Aviv. [*straightening as she faces them.*] He forced her even when she was impure.

TOVAH: [*shocked.*] During her period, her unclean days? Even to hand her a plate, to sit on the same couch is a terrible sin! To do the act, would sever your soul from God. You would lose your World to Come!

ADINA: Did the store help?

ZEHAVA: [*shaking her head no.*] He found others.

FRUME: Others?

GITTE LEAH: What do you mean? What "others"?

ZEHAVA: Other women. There was a woman he touched in a taxi on the way to B'nai Brak. She was going to go to the police. He sent Chana to talk her out of it. And then there was his mistress…

Total shock and disbelief.

CHANA: It went on for years. I followed him once. They would meet in a library. She was young, with bare arms and a pony-tail... She led him to a corner of the room. And when he kissed her, she took off his black hat and ran her fingers through his hair. I saw her wedding ring...

The circle stops. A bomb has fallen. SHEINHOFF *groans and collapses.* ADINA, FRUME, GITTE LEAH *attend her.*

ETA and TOVAH: Adultery. With a married woman? A crime deserving of death. *Gevalt!*

ZEHAVA: [*to all.*] Do you see now? Years she covered for him. For your sake, for the children's .... .

GITTE LEAH: She's desperate, and her Sephardi "friend" will say anything..

ETA: [*confused. Distancing herself from* CHANA.] I don't know what to believe anymore!

TOVAH: [*same. Piously.*] Even if what she says is true, it's a sin to listen to such evil talk.

CHANA: When it was about me, you listened. But when it's about my husband, a man, suddenly you don't want to hear. This is what my husband did! Already at the beginning of our marriage he asked all kinds of things from me.... physical things.... I was so innocent, I didn't understand I had a right to refuse. That my body belonged to me.... Every time I think of it, I want to die.

SHEINHOFF *takes out a prayer book with trembling hands. To lose herself in prayer, to stop the flow of information that is destroying her world.*

FRUME: How can you speak like this in front of your innocent daughters?

CHANA: [*with effort.*] I was also innocent once.... Forgive me, Mameh Goldie. I never wanted to hurt you. [SHEINHOFF *prays as if possessed.* CHANA *turns to her daughters.*] Girls...

BLUMA: [*to* CHANA.] I don't believe a single word you say. Our father is a ...a saint. Our father is pure!

CHANA: Did I ever lie to you? Didn't I teach you to lie was to go against God?

SHAINE RUTH: But you say everything was a lie! Your whole life, your marriage!

Beat. A moment of truth.

CHANA: Yes, I lived a lie. But as God is my witness, I'm telling you the truth now. Yankele Sheinhoff—the saint, the diligent, modest God-fearing scholar—was my invention. I created him. Please, Bluma, Shaine Ruth. You were both there that day. You know I'm not lying....

GITTE LEAH: [*to* CHANA.] Leave them be! It's enough! Enough of your sick fantasies and inventions. Come girls, let's go. Let's leave the crazy woman alone here with her friend. We have husbands and homes to take care of.

BLUME, SHAINE RUTH *are torn.* GITTE LEAH *pushes them.* SHEINHOFF, *in her own world, continues to pray hoarsely, intensely.*

TOVAH: Come Eta, I have to prepare the ritual baths for the evening.

ETA: And my husband will soon be home soon, and I haven't even peeled the potatoes....

CHANA: [*shouting.*] If you go, you will break your sacred oath!! You will forfeit your portion in the World to Come!

A terrified silence descends. This is a real threat. The circle holds them all, except for SHEINHOFF, *who gathers her strength and attempts to leave.*

ADINA: Mother! We swore! It's forbidden for any of us to leave until we come to a decision.

SHEINHOFF: I never took any oath, and I'm leaving. I've heard enough.

CHANA: [*surprised.*] Mameh Goldie, you took the holy Bible...

SHEINHOFF: I took nothing. What? Take an oath against my own child?!

ADINA: Mother, don't leave!

SHEINHOFF: I know my son better than any of you! I raised him. He wouldn't do such things.... My son is pure...my son is innocent...[*the prayer book falls from her hands. She bends to lift it. Kisses it with piety. Her legs wobble beneath her.*]

ADINA: [*in a whisper.*] Mother, you know that isn't true!

SHEINHOFF: [*denying.*] My son is pure like his father before him.

ADINA: [*in growing anger.*] It isn't true, Mother. It's a lie! Don't you remember what happened in the yeshiva?

SHEINHOFF: [*equally angry.*] What happened? Nothing happened! Child's play. A game....

ADINA: A game?! A child's game!? May God forgive me, I have no choice. [*loudly, to all.*] Years ago when my brother was learning in the yeshiva the principal caught him with another boy in the bathroom...The boy's parents threatened to call the police...

Shock and surprise. SHEINHOFF *continues to go, clutching her hair, her clothes.*

SHEINHOFF: Those parents misunderstood! They were fools. It was just a foolish game between youngsters.

ADINA: [*to all.*] He was thrown out of the yeshiva.

SHEINHOFF: [*like a lioness.*] It's not true, Adina! Yankele himself asked to transfer to another yeshiva. No one threw him out!

FRUME: What is Adina talking about?

GITTE LEAH: She says Yankele was thrown out of the yeshiva....

FRUME: How? When?!

ETA: Oy, a disgrace! A scandal!

TOVAH: What was that about the yeshiva? I didn't understand....

ADINA: If your family would have investigated, you would have found out. But who investigates such a well-connected bridegroom from such an honorable family. And our [*with irony*] *honorable* family did everything we could to hide it from the bride's family...

SHEINHOFF: Keep quiet!

ADINA: You have to defend him, Mother, I understand that. But Chana is also family. Why should she have to continue sacrificing herself? Hasn't she taken his black deeds on herself for enough years, so that he could play the saint? Admit it, Mother! The time has come for all of us to cleanse ourselves of his sins!

SHEINHOFF: Don't you dare say a bad word about him! He gave me grandchildren, and *nachas* (pride), and what have you done? Rejected one perfectly good marriage offer after another for no good reason. So it's better for you to hold your tongue, Adina, the way I've held mine all these years. I've dragged your shame around with me like a disease, like a hump on my back, eating myself up alive. Crying and holding my tongue, guarding your honor because you are my daughter. So now you hold your tongue, Adina! For once in your life, do something for your family!

Continues to leave, and is almost successful.

ADINA: He did the same thing to me!

Pause. SHEINHOFF *stops. The circle freezes. The shock of revelation is unbearable.*

ADINA: He…did the same thing to me.

SHEINHOFF: [*beats her chest with a closed fist. Keening.*] "For I have sinned, transgressed, perverted, been criminal…" [*taken from the* Yom Kippur *prayer*].

ADINA: Haven't you ever asked yourself why I don't marry? Why I reject suitor after suitor? Because I don't want to live with a lie in my soul, to deceive some decent young bridegroom, to pretend my whole life. Yes, I heard you crying at night Mother, but I choked back the words and held my tongue the way you always taught me women should…. But it's not possible anymore. Too many lives have been destroyed. Chana's, the children's, mine…

Heavy silence. SHEINHOFF *keens silently.*

SHEINHOFF: [*after a long silence.*] *Oy* to me and to my life…

ADINA: This is the truth about your son, my brother. This is my dowry…

SHEINHOFF: Adina-leh. What have we done to you? My child. *Mein Kinde, Mein Tireh* (my child, my dearest). How is it I didn't see? How did I let it happen? Why didn't you tell me? My child…. my child.

ADINA: Who would you have believed, Mother? Yankele or me? Look what happened to Chana when she told the truth.

SHEINHOFF: With my own hands, I will strangle him…. Chana, what have we done to you? Oh, Frume, what are we doing to our daughters? [*gathering strength.*] I want to take my oath now.

Waves off her daughter's help, and finds the Bible herself, and turns with it to face CHANA.

SHEINHOFF: I, Goldie Sheinhoff, widow of the saintly ADMOR of Lushiv, do swear to listen honestly and judge righteously. Chana Kashman was a wonderful mother. She is more than worthy to see her children. She is free of any blame. I vote yes. Let Chana see her children.

BLUMA: *Ima*, I'm so sorry. You deserve to see the children. [*they hug.*]

SHAINE RUTH: I also agree, *Ima*. I missed you so much. [*runs into her arms and hugs her.*]

ETA: We're sorry, Chana.

TOVAH: We were so afraid. Everyone was against you.

ETA, TOVAH: We also vote "yes".

Pause. Looking at FRUME.

FRUME: [*entrapped. In a small voice.*] How can we? How can we go against Rav Aaron? I can't do it! One word from him, and our family is destroyed in the community forever!

SHEINHOFF: How can we go against the will of our just and righteous God, Frume Kashman?

Pause. FRUME *realizes her choice.*

FRUME: Chana, perhaps I too was mistaken. Perhaps I punished you for the sins of others. I didn't understand. I didn't know.... Forgive me. Grant me *mechillah* (atonement).

CHANA: After I see my children.

FRUME: Go then. And may God help us both.

CHANA: Thank you, Mother.

ADINA: Gitte Leah, it's your turn.

GITTE LEAH *folds into herself in a corner.*

ADINA: Gitte Leah, for once in your life, say "yes" to the truth. There is no more room under the carpet. Give your little sister a chance to see her children.

GITTE LEAH *turns her back to* CHANA, *like a frightened child.*

FRUME: [*going to her.*] Come, Gitte Leah. *I* am asking you. Your sister is waiting.

GITTE LEAH: My sister. My sister. What about *me*? How will *I* go home? You know the ADMOR will never forgive me for siding with her...

FRUME: I will go with you. Together we will explain to him that we did our duty. That we made a judgment that was righteous and honest. Come, my child....

GITTE LEAH: [*last appeal.*] You can't forgive Chana. If you do, all my sacrifices, all I've suffered, was for nothing! You think I didn't want to run away from my husband, my life? (*in pain*) Mother....

FRUME: What hurts you? Is it your back again?

GITTE LEAH: My heart, Mother. It's my heart....

CHANA: Gitte Leah, am I allowed to see my children?

GITTE LEAH: [*whisper.*] You are allowed. Go in peace.

CHANA: Thank you, sister.

> *They approach each other, but cannot bridge the gap that will allow them to hug. Pause.*

SHAINE RUTH: The vote is over. It's unanimous. Our mother—that is—Chana Kashman, is allowed to see her children.

CHANA: Finally. My daughters [*embracing them and sobbing.*] "From the depths I cried out to Him and He answered me..."

ZEHAVA: I never believed you'd win! ...You've won. [*embraces her.*]

CHANA: How often I dreamed of this!

SHEINHOFF: [*in the meantime, dialing the phone.*] Hello? Yes Rabbi... [*corrects herself*] yes Mister Aaron. This is Goldie Sheinhoff. *Rebbitzen* Sheinhoff. No, no we haven't gotten rid of her. The opposite. We already know the truth and now we're going to bring her to the children. Don't threaten me, Aaron. Have you no fear of heaven in you at all? You or your hooligans? Yes, so what will you do? Break *my* hands and feet, the hands and feet of all the women here? [*beat.*] *You* don't frighten me. I'm afraid of only one thing: The Holy One Blessed be He. [*slams down the phone.*] Come, Chana, let's go. The children are waiting.

> *The phone rings again, it rings and rings, but no one bothers to answer.*

WOMEN *and* CHANA *are poised to leave.*

SHAINE RUTH: We have to ...

BLUMA: Wait, there's something...

CHANA: [*dismissing their concerns with a smile.*] You'll tell me after. After I hold my baby Shifra in my arms again. After I bury my face in her neck and breathe in that baby smell once more. After I kiss her fingers, one by one...and she laughs and laughs. My baby.... Then I'll bring them all back here and we'll all sit around the table and talk, me in my place, as if it was the Sabbath, and you'll all understand that not for a moment, a second, did I stop loving any of you...

Everyone exits. BLUMA *and* SHAINE RUTH *linger behind looking at each other. They too exit. Off.*

FRUME'S VOICE: Quiet! Move out of our way. Have you no respect for honorable Jewish women, you criminals? Get out of here. Go back to your yeshivas, you still have a lot to learn! Oh, how did I dare open such a mouth against the men...!

Epilogue

The stage becomes a street. Large street posters hung on the walls warn women to dress properly, to act in accordance with community dictates. Graffiti against CHANA *in red paint call her a whore, and say her punishment will come.*

BLUMA *and* SHAINE RUTH *enter, hiding in the corner on the street.* CHANA *enters from the opposite direction. She is traumatized.*

BLUMA: *Ima...*

CHANA: Their eyes—oh God! Their eyes! So cold...[*frozen, her voice dry and cracked.*] Moishele looked at me as if I was a monster. And Ruchele cried when I came near her, as if I had come to eat her alive. Eliahu couldn't catch his breath...

BLUMA: Rav Aaron told us to tell the children that Satan had taken you away. And the proof was—

SHAINE RUTH:—that if they looked you in the eyes, they'd die.

CHANA: [*heartbroken, and yet relieved.*] Ah! I see.

The girls murmur apologies, asking forgiveness.

SHAINE RUTH: They aren't to blame. It's not their fault.

CHANA: [*tiredly.*] No. It's my fault. Granny Frume was right. Children are not a suitcase you can put down and pick up. It's late. The children need to come home and be put to bed. I must leave here.

BLUMA: Where will you go?

CHANA: Don't worry about me, Bluma. Take care of the family you're building...

SHAINE RUTH: Really Bluma?

CHANA: Good-bye, my girls.

SHAINE RUTH: *Ima,* Wait! Please, don't go! Bluma, we can't let her go like that! [BLUMA *shrugs. To* CHANA.] What will happen to you?

CHANA: I'll live somehow. Don't forget I love you, always. And take care of the little ones. Try to explain to them. In time, maybe a miracle will happen and our people will learn to have the same compassion as our God.... Good-bye my darlings. [*the girls both cling to her.*] And may God deal kindly with you both.

SHAINE RUTH: [*refusing to accept.*] *Ima,* wait! I'm going with you.

BLUMA: Shaine Ruth, you can't! You have to stay. Without *Aba* or Rav Aaron, who will arrange for your marriage?

SHAINE RUTH: [*in revulsion.*] Do you think, Bluma, after everything I've heard I'd let those two men choose a husband for me?

CHANA: Shaine Ruth, your sister is right. I have no money. No place to live. I'm an outcast. You're better off staying with your father and his family....

SHAINE RUTH: [*determined, quoting from the Book of Ruth.*] "Whither thou goest, I will go. Wither thou lodgest, I will lodge. Thy people will be my people and thy God, my God!"

CHANA: [*embracing her.*] My child!

CHANA *and* SHAINE RUTH *exit.* BLUMA *is left alone. The street is full of noises. The men's voices call out epithets, demands. Looking at the posters telling her how she must live her life, she re-enters her world with full knowledge and disappears.*

CURTAIN

About the Author

Naomi Ragen

Naomi Ragen is the author of several international best-sellers, among them *Jephte's Daughter, Sotah, The Sacrifice of Tamar, The Ghost of Hannah Mendes, Chains on the Grass,* and *The Covenant.* Born in New York, she earned a BA from Brooklyn College and an MA in English from the Hebrew University of Jerusalem. For the past thirty years, she has made her home in Jerusalem. The translation of her books into Hebrew in 1995 has made her one of Israel's best-beloved authors. An outspoken advocate for gender equality and human rights, she contributes to numerous periodicals, including *The Jerusalem Post, The Miami Herald,* and *Moment Magazine.* Ragen's hit play *Women's Minyan,* commissioned by Israel's National Theater, Habimah, has been running for two years, and her weekly e-mail columns on life in the Middle East are read and distributed by thousands of subscribers worldwide.

The author welcomes reader comments and can be contacted at POB 23004, Jerusalem 91230, Israel, or through email: Naomi@ NaomiRagen.com

The fonts used in this book are from the Garamond family

Other works by Naomi Ragen
published by *The* Toby Press

NOVELS

The Sacrifice of Tamar

Jephte's Daughter

Sotah

Chains Around the Grass

The Toby Press publishes fine writing,
available at leading bookstores everywhere. For more
information, please visit www.tobypress.com